THE WOUNDS
OF HUNGER

THE WOUNDS
OF HUNGER

A NOVEL BY LUIS SPOTA

TRANSLATED AND EDITED BY
BARNABY CONRAD

HOUGHTON MIFFLIN COMPANY BOSTON
THE RIVERSIDE PRESS CAMBRIDGE · 1957

• 25599

Más cornadas da el hambre que los toros
Hunger wounds worse than the bulls

SPANISH SAYING ATTRIBUTED TO
THE MATADOR "EL ESPARTERO"

Foreword by Barnaby Conrad

LET ME SAY STRAIGHT OFF THAT THIS IS THE most powerful bullfighting novel I have ever read.

On the jacket of the Mexican edition, where it was first published in 1949, the Manuel Porrua Press wrote: "This novel is as hard, rough, bitter and brutal as life itself . . ."

The distinguished critic of Mexico City's *El Universal*, Rafael Solana, said last year in writing of the book's great success in France: "There is no doubt about it, Luis Spota is one of Mexico's greatest novelists, no matter how he may shock you. I always considered *Les Bestiares* of Montherlant the best bullfighting novel ever written; it looks like sentimental hogwash next to Spota's book. Hemingway's writing on the bulls is good. Spota's is better."

For the first time the wretched struggle which lies behind

the glamorous *fiesta brava* has been truly depicted; it is not pretty, the people are not lovely, but this is the way it is in Mexico and that is the way Luis Spota has written it. I'm not sure that I would have encouraged the publication of this book ten years ago; at that time not enough people in the United States were aware of the spectacle's irresistible qualities to be told of its many indefensible ones. But since then there have been many books and moving pictures and magazine articles extolling the glamour of *los toros*, and in cocktail chatter in New York, Chicago, San Francisco or Los Angeles, it is quite common to hear such words and names as *verónica*, *aficionado*, Dominguín, Manolete, and so forth. All over this country now there are clubs which collect and share news of the bull world, their members being of all ages and from all walks of life. So now, with the glories of tauromachy so entrenched in American letters and culture, it is perhaps time to show the less pleasant aspects of the science. And Luis Spota is the man to do it.

I first came in contact with this novel when I was in Mexico City working with Carlos Arruza on his autobiography. I took it back to San Francisco, read it, became excited about it, and shortly thereafter returned to Mexico to meet the author and arrange for its translation into English. An attractive, friendly, intense, pipe-smoking gentleman of thirty-two, Luis Spota looks more like an assistant professor of history at the University of California than a worldly citizen of Mexico City. He has written eleven books, most of them on the seamier side of Mexican life, and *The Wounds of Hunger*, written when he was twenty-three, is his favorite. In its original edition the book has sold over 50,000 copies. Only recently published in other languages, it has already had a great success in France under the title *C'est l'Heure, Matador.*

Luis Spota aspired to be a matador, and since he went

through an apprenticeship much like the one Luis Ortega suffers through, there is an unmistakable ring of authenticity in every chapter of this book. There is no trace here of the *españolada* — the Hollywood-type conception of matadors and bullfighting so painful and insulting to Mexicans and Spaniards.

Kenneth Tynan, in his good book *Bull Fever*, has written:

"One of the bullfight's greatest enemies is the intense romantic. It is in many ways a pity that most of the books which have brought bullfighting to the English language (I except Hemingway's, still the soundest and best) have been written in a state of literary *kif:* 'A dark, swelling knot tightened within José's gut. This was it, then, this was what men called fear and he looked away. Mother of God, he needed another *anís*, how bad he needed it. His gut was a flapping, empty wineskin, like a man should not have if he is killing bulls. And he was out there alone with it, alone with the horned fury. Little Saint Penelope of the lollipops, but that Number 28 was an *ayuntamiento* with sabres, a bitch of a bull. I got to tie the bastard down, crooned José within himself, I got to make a beauty of the bastard . . . "Uhh-hah, Señor Toro, I am ready for you, you chicken-pellet," said José el Rubio, and he straightened his old man's shoulders and he took the black bulk of the most noble bull of all the Conde's pastures full on the point of his singing sword. "Was it well done?" he shouted to his peasant of confidence. "Was it well done, Pepe?" And Pepe showed him his young man's thumb and said that yes, it was well done, it was well done indeed . . .' "

You will not find this sort of nonsense in Spota; his writing is stark and bare and so absent of style that its very absence becomes style of a sort. He simply wants to get a thought or an action over to his reader in the most direct way possible, no frills, no embroidery, no *filigranas*.

In spite of Luis Ortega's one-dimensionalness, I was interested in his and his companions' fate from the very beginning of the book to the very end. I think it was because I *believed* in him and the other characters so completely; I never felt that their lives were being manipulated by an author, but rather that they were simply being recorded.

For example, take that business where they are in Fresnillo and with luck and skill Camioneto manages to talk the priest into putting Luis on the program for the fight that Sunday. After all the build-up and preparations you are positive that this corrida is going to be very important in Luis's life one way or another. But what happens? The author has no control over his characters, they are breathing, independent entities, for though it would be very nice for both the reader and the author to see what would happen in that fight and how Luis would do, the fight doesn't even come off! Luis gets into a scrape over a woman and has to get out of town fast, never again to return. Spota has that quality of making you believe in the actions of his characters even if you do not necessarily love them.

The novel starts in Mexico City and for a year we travel around the states of Mexico with Luis and Camioneto before coming full circle, like Quixote and Sancho, back to where we started. After these travels with their picaresque adventures the reader knows a great deal more about bullfighting, about the Mexican people, and about life than he did before he set out. It is a hard journey, sometimes shocking, often naïve, frequently exciting, occasionally touching, and you will never find the route in Baedeker. But it is worth the trip, and I urge you to take it.

B.C.

THE WOUNDS
OF HUNGER

1

OBVIOUSLY, THIS WAS IT. LUIS ORTEGA
glanced again at the tired piece of paper, scarred and seamed
from its foldings, to read the same letters as were over the
door:

CAFÉ CANTONÉS

The paper said "Bolívar Street," and that's where they
were, with their greasy caps pulled down to their ears. Pancho
Camioneto studied it, the visor of his cap askew.

"What do you say — shall we go in?"

He looked like some sort of wild animal, with his hair curling over his ears and his black darting eyes, his Indian features. Luis, by comparison, was good-looking, being taller,
lighter of skin, and possessed of a pair of sunken eyes of an

incredible green. He was seventeen, almost two years younger than Camioneto.

"You go first," said Luis.

"You're the matador."

"You're the manager," answered Luis.

Under his blue cotton shirt, under the undernourished skin which sheathed his ribs, Luis's heart was giving little erratic thumps, the same painful way it did before going out to give a bull the first pass. Or when, in front of the horns, his mouth was dry of saliva and his tongue was a large rough sponge.

"Into the arena, Matador!" said Pancho, pushing open the glass doors for Luis.

He hesitated a moment. His hands had begun to sweat. Lord, it was the first time in his life that he'd been inside a café in Mexico City — and a bullfighting café at that! In his home town he'd dreamt of this magic place where one talked of hopes and glory and money and women and of great afternoons. Now he would see it.

They went in. Luis stopped at the second step. In front of him, like a drab hallway, the narrow café stretched out. On both sides dark wooden booths. In the middle, grubby tables. On the walls covered with dust and spiderwebs were advertisements for soda pop, a mirror in a gilt frame, and a drab chrome of the gardens of Xochimilco. And of bullfighting, nothing. Not even one of the bad paintings that one saw everywhere else.

The air in the place was sour, like the breath from a mouth whose teeth have never been brushed. A pasty-faced China-man was arranging buns on a tray. Camioneto's eyes went to a nearby waitress's breasts.

"Who you looking for?" she asked. She'd never seen these boys, who were like all the other would-be toreros, and yet different.

Luis swallowed. "Rafaelillo."

She'd picked up the tray of buns. "There — that booth over there. You can follow me."

She turned and walked toward a far table surrounded by laughing youths.

"Come on — " Camioneto limped after the waitress and Luis followed.

The waitress put the tray on the table making room for it among the glasses of milky coffee, the empty plates of beans and fried eggs, and the bottles of lemonade. Luis and Camioneto had stayed a few steps behind.

Rafaelillo, laughing with his mouth full of food, was saying, " — and so I said to her, you got to go out with this type and bring me back some stuff, so when she said she wouldn't I slammed some knuckles into her face and chipped a couple of teeth for her. Great, eh?"

"Great," said the fat girl he had at his right.

Suddenly they grew quiet. Before them were two unknowns, two boys in sneakers, torn pants, shirts knotted at the waist, and caps. The two dusty boys smiled, timidly and briefly. Rafaelillo glanced at them disdainfully with his heavy-lidded eyes and started to resume his conversation. Then he slapped his hand on the table.

"But it's you!"

"Hola, Rafael," Luis stammered.

They stepped up to the edge of the table. Rafaelillo stood up and shook their hands. Rafael looked prosperous; his suit was gray cashmere and around his neck he wore a magenta silk scarf. He smelled of Pinaud cologne.

"Sit down — sit down — " he gestured. Turning to his friends he introduced them as "two artists of the bull ring."

The artists of the bull ring pulled up two chairs. Between their feet, because it was the safest place, Camioneto put the bundle which contained the ever present cape and muleta. Those sitting with Rafaelillo looked at them a moment with the same undisguised curiosity with which two penguins at the zoo might be observed, and then they returned to their own affairs.

"You — you know what?" Luis was nervous and ill at ease, and this always made him stammer. "We've been off fighting the 'wars' — the bullfighting wars — just got here to Mexico City — today. I've kept your address. Ever since you came through our town last year. That's why I came to — "

"You were lucky, boy." Rafaelillo took a mouthful, rinsed his mouth, and then spat the water out one side. "Lucky to catch me. I was just on my way."

"You fighting soon?" asked Pancho Camioneto.

"Don't know." Rafaelillo shrugged with studied casualness. "Matter of fact, tonight I'm going to see Don Paco, my manager. He'll tell me."

Someone had ordered a veal steak which the waitress now delivered. Camioneto's muddy brown eyes jabbed into the richly breaded meat like a fork. Rafael spotted the fleeting glimmer. Chewing on a pencil-thin Corona, he asked, "Feel like eating?"

Camioneto was going to say something, but Luis nudged him in the ribs.

"Thanks, mano," he said, using the short term for *hermano* — brother — and trying to be casual. "Not hungry yet."

It was Sunday and the café was beginning to fill up with people who were reading the *Redondel* or discussing Luis Procuna or Arruza or whether or not Velásquez could keep up his suicidal pace, or if Joselillo's style wasn't leading him straight to death.

Rafaelillo asked for the check and paid a twenty-peso bill. As he arose he left a fifty-centavo tip. Out of the corner of his eye Luis saw one of those at the table neatly and cleanly slip the tip off the table top and into a pocket.

"Got any plans?" Rafael asked as they left the place.

"We — we thought you might be able to help us," said Luis. "I've got to get a chance to fight, Rafael."

They crossed the street. The others said goodbye and went off, and now it was just Rafael and the two country boys. The novillero climbed into a Cadillac convertible. He started the motor.

"Well," he said, "we'll get together tomorrow. I work out every day at La Plaza México at nine. I'm going to see Don Paco now. I'll speak to him about you. He's got ways to do anything — with the impresario, newspapers, everywhere. To show you what he can do, look at me — " His thumbs caressed the undersides of his lapels of his gray jacket.

"Thanks," said Luis gratefully, "thanks, Rafael."

"See you in La México then — early."

The Cadillac turned off at the corner of Uruguay Street and disappeared. Now they were alone again without funds in the very center of the metropolis. They started walking.

The Café Do Brasil was swarming with noisy people. In front of it the Café Tupinaimba was a madhouse, everybody talking, nobody listening. They pressed their noses against the glass and for a long time they watched the incredible and fascinating human landscape within. On the sidewalk, like cactus growths of hungry flesh, dozens of young toreros as poor as they conversed, told lies to each other, or simply amused themselves by watching passers-by, those strange people who thought about normal things like work, or families, or payday, or debts or duties.

"Why're you so stupid?" said Camioneto.

Luis looked at him questioningly.

"When that guy asked you said no."

"And what was I supposed to say? That we're starving? That'd be pretty. If he'd been alone I'd have said sure. But with all those people — "

They went down the dark streets off Uruguay. In front

of the Hotel Bayona a woman made a sign to them. They smiled without stopping. "Women at this hour," said Ortega. He was hungry. "We haven't eaten," he calculated, "for thirty hours." Besides that they had to figure out where to sleep tonight. But the city was big and something would turn up. They reached the San Juan de Letrán intersection. On the corner, an old woman was hawking tender corn. The sweet hot aroma of the ears boiling in a pot assailed their nostrils and saliva filled their mouths.

"How much parné do we have left?" Luis asked, using the gypsy slang term for money. All the toreros used strange words, a language of their own, that he was trying hard to master. The smell of the fresh corn had re-awakened the pangs of hunger.

Under the light of an archway Camioneto counted the community funds. Three coppers showed up in his hand.

The corn woman was shouting that the ears were one peseta each.

With the coins in his hand, Luis went up to the woman and asked for an ear from the charcoal pot. The vendor was off her guard as she concentrated on finding one that would please her customer. Out of the corner of his eye, Luis watched Camioneto appropriate four fat ears and limp casually away. Luis paid for the one he had requested and then went quickly down the street after his friend.

He was waiting, seated on a bench. On his knees the bundle and on top of that three of the ears. His teeth were firmly in the fourth.

"If you're going to steal," said Camioneto with pride, "steal like an artist."

"No one's better at it," said Luis with a smile.

"Chile with salt? Got some of that too."

Luis shook his head admiringly. What a type, Camioneto.

Once, when Camioneto was younger, he wanted to be a torero, and he could have been. But he wasn't. He explained it in two sentences: "I lacked the guts, and I liked the women and the liquor too much. And then that business with that bull — "

"That business" was a common enough thing, an accident of the profession. In a fair at Jalisco a morucho — a rotten half-breed ox — had handed him a goring in the sciatic nerve and left him lame. That was all.

Luis Ortega finished the first ear of corn. His lips burned from the hot sauce and his stomach began to feel better. He started on the second. Camioneto was gorging himself like a jackal.

A filthy little newspaper boy had come near them. Swarthy, pot-bellied, ragged, he watched them with covetous black eyes without saying anything.

"What's doing, kid?" Luis started to give him a pat. The child pulled away without ceasing to look at the half-gnawed ear. Luis hesitated and looked at the corn. He looked at those eyes. Then he held it out. "Here."

Camioneto stopped in the middle of an enormous bite.

"Bruto! Here we hardly have enough for us and you go and hand it out!"

"I'm full."

"If you don't want it, stow it, but don't give it away. With all the trouble I go to keep us in food!"

"Where do we sleep?"

"We'll find a place."

Luis Ortega, Matador de Novillos, and Pancho Camioneto, Manager, sword handler and mentor, spent that first night in Mexico City wrapped up in a cape and muleta in the Garden of the Frog on the corner of Bolívar and Venustiano Carranza Streets.

2

HE REMAINED STILL FOR A FEW MINUTES WITH
his eyes open wide. Dawn hadn't broken and the city was
beginning to become populated with those mysterious beings
who give life to the daybreak. La Rompecatres — The Cot-
Breaker — the motherly prostitute of many a young torero
now a star, went by again towards Allende Street on the last
trip of the night. A streetcar left its ancient clang on some
far-off intersection; two drunks, leaning on each other, relieved themselves on the sidewalk in front of the Flower of
Mexico.

Luis stirred himself.

"Come on, let's go."

Camioneto's reply was a groan, and he wrapped himself
up tighter in the muleta. Luis kept at him. Camioneto shook
his head, pulled his cap down even with his eyebrows and
yawned.

"But it's still night! Don't muck around — let me sleep
a while longer."

Luis had stood up and picked up the big work cape: a
soiled hunk of cloth impregnated with horn wounds, dirt,
and dreams.

It meant a lot to him, that cape. Just before his mother
had died she had called Luis to her in their miserable adobe
hovel. She was dying of some disease with a difficult name
that made her flesh smell terribly. Luis went up to the cot
where she lay, a sunken-faced heap of bones. "Good boy — "

she had gasped, "— always good boy. Tin can — behind brick — pesos — buy something — something you want — before I die — so I can see you happy." He had bought the battle-scarred cape from one of Rafaelillo's banderilleros when they had come through his town last year. He had shown it to his mother and told her he was going to become a torero with it and make lots of money for her. She was too sick to protest except with her eyes.

Now he folded it carefully and tucked it under his arm.

"Look." He pointed up at the clock. "It's past five."

"But Rafael said we wouldn't see him till nine."

"The plaza is a long way off and we're walking. We'll barely make it."

Camioneto finally stood up. His stomach was a crater of hunger. He spat bitterly. He put his hand in his pocket to scratch himself.

"Let them eat," Luis mocked, "Or buy yourself some calomel."

"You're worse than the crabs. Bitching all the time."

San Juan de Letrán Avenue was gray and cold. The high buildings were geometric clouds of gray cement and they became blended with the vaporous smoke of the fog. From somewhere came the first light of a sleepy sun. "Why does the sun get up so goddamn early?" Camioneto said. "Jesus, am I hungry." He spat bitterly again.

"And the parné?"

"Got it here. There's — " Ortega recounted it, "a twenty left."

"Two buns, at least."

"Yeh, at least."

They asked a policeman, sleeping standing up in his blue mackinaw, how to get to the Plaza México. He said to grab the first bus marked Colonia Del Valle on 16th of September Street. Camioneto smiled.

"Sure, or take a taxi. But it appears we're walking. If we had the fare we'd be breakfasting."

"I guess so," said the policeman. "What are you, anyway?"

"Toreros," Luis answered.

"Ah! Toreros! The plaza is out there — "

With their hands deep in their pockets, their arms tight in against their thin, coatless bodies, the young toreros set out walking along San Juan. A squad car with its lights on passed by slowly. Then a drunk and painted floozy. Inside the Café Cristal there were still a few clients. They hesitated at the door, looking inside, and then they glanced at each other. No, with twenty centavos they couldn't even get any plate leavings in there.

The sun had come out completely when they arrived at Avenida Insurgentes. In the distance among the surrounding morning grayness, they made out the gigantic funnel that is the Plaza México, its upper part painted a sunny cream color.

"There it is!" breathed Luis, and upon saying it he felt a shiver of excitement.

Half running they covered the remaining distance. The great jutting colosseum seemed about to press down and crush them. Dully, awed, they circled it, gazing at the life-size statues of different matadors on the pillars that made up the fence around the ring, and the bronze herd of bulls over the main portal.

The iron gate was locked. Camioneto banged on it authoritatively. Minutes went by. Then on the other side of the bars there appeared the dirty, puffy face of the watchman.

"What you want?" he barked.

"What do you think? To come in."

"For what?"

"To work out. We're toreros."

The man studied them, shaking his head. He showed his teeth and turned his back.

"But we're novilleros!"

"Who says so?" The watchman had turned around with a snarl. "I don't know you. Besides, you have to have a pass."

"From whom?"

"From the impresario."

He turned away, deaf to any further talk. They crossed the street and sat down on a bench. With his chin in his hands, Luis said:

"What a plaza, eh? Some day, some Sunday at three-thirty we'll walk in there, you and I, Camioneto, right through that door. Me, dressed in a suit of lights — "

"When?"

"Soon, mano, soon. Before long, as soon as they get to know me, they'll come up with a corrida for me. Just once. Then they'll see!"

Camioneto entered into the enjoyment of the fantasy.

"Where would you want the bulls to be from?"

Luis Ortega shrugged his shoulders. "Any place. You know when a man's a real torero it doesn't matter what ranch they come from. Just let them charge hard, that's all."

"Olé!"

"All I ask is that they charge hard and fast. I'll take care of the rest."

When a Cadillac stopped in front of the gate and the driver blew his horn imperiously, the young toreros stood up. They saw the profile of a young man, almost as young as they, seated behind the wheel. He was well dressed, and a streak of white on the right side of his head relieved the shiny blackness of his hair.

They recognized him immediately.

"It's Luis Procuna!"

The watchman appeared and upon seeing the car immediately swung back the gate. The boys stuck their heads in the window.

"Matador," pleaded Luis Ortega, "give us a break."

"What's this?" frowned Procuna.

"That bum there —" Camioneto pointed with the black nail of his index finger — "he's gotten flamenco on us and won't let us in. We're toreros and we just arrived yesterday from the small-town wars — we don't know anybody here."

He saw how anxiously they awaited an answer, how awed they were by the luxury of his clothes and his car. He called over the watchman.

"They're with me."

Luis's heart leapt.

"Gracias, Matador," he exclaimed as Procuna drove on.

They walked in, gaping at the corrals, the little chapel, the dressing rooms for the picadors and banderilleros. Then they went in the tunnel — a sluice of darkness that led towards the cuadrilla gate. As he went down it, Luis was imagining that this wasn't a chilly early morning now, but rather a moment between three and four of a Sunday afternoon, and he was dressed in a suit of lights of white and gold, like a prince, with a rich dress cape embroidered by La Maestra slung over his left shoulder and the montera hat pressed firmly down to his eyebrows; and on the other side of the unknown there awaited a crowd of forty thousand people who would set up a thunderous roar the moment he set foot out on the gold sand of the arena.

When they came up and leaned over the red barrier fence, Procuna was already running around the ring fast; then he began some push-ups. Afterwards he practiced running forward and backward. Then he went through some graceful ring maneuvers.

"Look." Camioneto wasn't missing a single detail of the famous torero's exercises. "A millionaire but look at him working out, staying in shape. And if he does it, him, a big star now, imagine what you're going to have to do!"

Even empty, the plaza was overpowering. The stands were littered with papers, peels, sun shades, paper cups from the previous afternoon. One of these fine days, Luis thought, I'm going to fill this place up to the brim — not a ticket left.

"Sí señor," Camioneto was going on, "and every Sunday he makes fifty thousand pesos, easy."

"I'll make that much too, if they just give me a chance."

"But get one thing straight," Pancho Camioneto emphasized. "To get to be a torero there's only one road: close to the horns. The cars, the clothes, the eats three times a day, the houses, the women, the applause, the friends — they're right there between the bull's withers. They're sitting there for anyone to grab, but nobody who isn't hung right gets them."

"I got the guts, you know that," answered Luis, seated now on the stirrup board that runs around the fence inside the ring.

"It's not just a question of guts, Luis. As I always say, as they all say, you got to throw some brains at the bull, not just guts. How many of us have had it at first and then messed it all up the second time around! Thousands of us — "

"Not me."

"I'm going to damn well see to it. You're either coming out a torero or you're coming out feet first."

A skinny, pale boy, beardless and with a crooked face, came up to them. Silently he sat next to them. His dark and timid eyes deep in their hollows studied the famous torero. Like Luis and Camioneto, the other boy had a muleta under his arm. He looked at the cape of the country boys.

"How about a faena?" he inquired timidly.

"Let's go."

"I don't have a capote — if you could lend — "

"Sure."

They got up. The newcomer volunteered to be the bull if they'd be one for him afterwards. The charges began. Uncertainly, as though he were in front of a real bull, Luis Ortega gave ground on the first lunges.

"Stand still!" Camioneto lashed out from his place along the fence. "Hold it, for God's sake!"

Ortega, upon hearing the cry, changed his style. His body straightened, he threw out his chest and he swung his arms — one, two, three — up to six times. Then he finished off with a half-verónica.

He was learning the recipe for the perfect verónica, according to the café gospel:

"The cape dragging; the hands low; the off leg out front, the waist, muy torero; the chin in rhythm, going along with the charge. And whenever possible the big bill in the wallet and a small bull in the ring."

His work with the muleta was serious, calm. As though practicing a ritual, Luis Ortega moved his wrists, giving life to the red rag hung on the short stick. The boy who was playing the part of the bull let himself be lined up, his head low. The matador profiled himself, cocked his leg, and lunged in after the imaginary sword to execute a perfect kill.

"Ooooléee, Matador!" Pancho Camioneto's shout echoed in the empty plaza.

At eleven, the Aguascalientes boy took his muleta, wished them good luck and left. Procuna had gone off in his Cadillac. Other toreros and would-be toreros kept arriving. The ring was filled with characters of every type, from an elegant and cologned senior matador to the worst bum, even worse off than the two country boys. It was hot and Luis felt his legs giving way from fatigue and hunger. He sat down on the stirrup board. If he just had a cigarette at least to stave off the gnawing in his belly! Of course he could clamp on to the water faucet and fill himself up. But that was bad for the body, especially while working out. He decided to stay sitting on the stirrup board.

"I think that bastard isn't coming." Camioneto was looking up at the clock way up in the sunny section of the stands. It was eleven-thirty.

Luis's heart sank.

Finally Rafaelillo, his jaunty silk scarf knotted around his throat, appeared in the gate of cuadrillas. On aching legs the country boys went eagerly across the ring to greet him.

"Got hung up," said the novillero. "Bring your things?"

They showed him the patched cape and muleta. Rafaelillo looked at them, picking the cape up disdainfully.

"Sure you couldn't find any crappier ones?"

"It's a good cape," Luis said defensively.

Rafaelillo asked Luis to be the bull. He agreed in spite of his faintness and fatigue. When the faena was finished, after more talking than fighting, Rafael said he was worn out and hung over.

"Let's quit, before I kick off right here," he said, wiping his sweaty neck.

They went back up to his car. At an alarming speed they drove away through the streets to Insurgentes Avenue. They drove by the Reforma monument. Ortega was seeing the city for the first time. Never had he seen so many beautiful and tall buildings, nor so many cars and so many well-dressed people.

The convertible's tires squeaked on the asphalt as it swung around the statue of Carlos IV and hurled itself into the thick of the traffic of Rosales. It turned around Colón and jerked to a stop near the back door of the Regis Hotel.

"Going to take a Turkish bath." Rafael turned off the motor and put the keys in his pocket. "Last night I really hung one on — I'm raw as a radish. Been with a woman until now and I'm worn down, dead. I just went to the plaza for you two."

When they were alone, Luis started thinking about what Rafael had just said. He couldn't understand, in the brief experiences of his seventeen years, how a star novillero like his friend could abuse his physical condition like that with liquor and the other business.

"How about that, Pancho? Can a torero think about women and liquor and partying and bulls all at the same time?"

Camioneto shoved his cap back on his head with his thumb.

"It can't be. For a torero the bottle and a skirt are more dangerous than the bull. Either you think about screwing or you think about bullfighting. Not both."

And Luis Ortega agreed that's the way it must be, since Camioneto knew about things better than anyone.

A while afterwards, Rafaelillo reappeared. They got out of the car. The novillero was transformed: fresh, smelling of cologne, apparently free from the nagging hangover.

"Rafael," Luis stammered as they got out of the car. "Did you talk to Don Paco?"

"Ah, yes. Last night I told him about you. Wants to meet you. Particularly you, since you're the matador." He took a card from his wallet and scribbled a dozen words on it. "Go see him and — and handle him right. He's a good old boy and he can sure take care of you!"

He was about to start off when Camioneto stepped forward. "Matador, could you slip us a little loan? We're broke and haven't eaten for a week — "

Rafaelillo smiled. He knew how it was. Money lent to a torero is money thrown out the window. He shook his head. "I'm in the same fix, broke. If I weren't, be glad to — you understand, eh?"

3

AFTER THEY HAD RUNG TWICE THE DOOR was opened. A thin dark youth asked what they wanted.

"To see Don Paco. Rafaelillo sent us — " He delivered the card.

The door was closed again. It was one of the big houses in the Juárez district. Two blocks to the right they'd spotted a grove of poplars with a fountain in the middle. They arrived there after asking a dozen people. The beardless youth returned to let them in.

"He'll be right here," he said and disappeared into a room.

Luis and Camioneto waited in the tiled foyer. The only furniture was a wicker sofa.

Suddenly there appeared a tall and very thin man, with a sharp, pale face, blue in its unshavenness. When he opened his mouth to inquire which was Luis Ortega, there was the shaggy odor of decaying teeth.

"I am, Don Paco," said Luis, trying to stand even straighter.

He studied the boy from head to feet. He stared at the lean, young face, the high cheekbones, the eyes that were decent and still not hard, in spite of the hard things they had seen. He nodded at Camioneto inquiringly.

"My friend — he helps me, trains me," said Luis. "Cami oneto."

"Camioneto?" said Don Paco distastefully. "What a name!

"Before I started to fight, I drove a truck — a camión. S they call me Camioneto."

Don Paco gestured for them to sit down on the sofa. H sat down next to Luis. He put one of his bony hands on Luis knee in a fatherly fashion. He smiled.

"So you want to be a torero, eh?"

"Yes, Don Paco."

"Got guts? Hung right?"

Luis nodded. Camioneto interrupted graphically with hi hands.

"Like a bull's."

"We'll see, we'll see," said the manager of matadors. H stood up and the two boys followed suit.

He signaled to Luis. "Come with me. And you, Camioneto you wait."

They went into a small room with a very high ceilin fancily wallpapered. The office, explained Don Paco. Ther was an ancient sofa and an ornate desk. On the walls, dozer of photos of toreros. Above the doorway glowered th mounted head of a black bull with vicious horns.

"Got any programs or photos?" asked Don Paco, lettin himself drop into an overstuffed chair.

"No, Don Paco."

"In the union?"

"No."

He shook his head.

"Bad, bad, especially since you're an unknown. You alwa have to show programs and photos to the impresario."

"You know how it is, Don Paco — in the country wars t important thing is to get to fight, not to get pictures taken

Don Paco laughed.

"And it's the same here, my lad. Far as I'm concerned there are two types of toreros: Those that bullfight the public and those who bullfight the bull." Then he said abruptly: "Eaten?"

"No, Don Paco."

"Fine, they'll give you something here, and to your friend. But —" he stood up, and his hands felt Luis's arms, back and waist — "you're really thin. Have to fatten you up. Otherwise the day you get into a suit of lights you're going to look like a toothpick." He gave him a friendly little push into an adjoining room. "Now, take a bath. There's still some hot water. I'll give you a shirt. Strip!"

When Don Paco had left, Luis began to wonder why the devil this man wanted him to bathe. He put his nostrils down to an armpit. It wasn't that bad. Well, as Rafaelillo said, you had to let the old goat have his way.

He was in a bedroom. He opened the other door. There was the tub of shiny porcelainized metal, a toilet, a basin, and another fixture he'd never seen before and couldn't imagine what it might be used for: a bidet.

He peeled off his shirt and his tennis shoes, but kept on his drawers. Don Paco came back with a white article of clothing in hands which he placed on the bed.

"Shirt," said Don Paco. Then seeing Luis still in his shorts, "Come on, strip!"

Ortega obeyed, a little embarrassed having to do it in front of this man who'd kept looking at him with a little smile. He got in the tub and turned the faucet. The water was lukewarm.

"Your friend," said Don Paco, leaning on the door, "is out here really piling it on for my boys. According to him you're only the greatest torero that ever was born."

With his face full of soap, Luis said apologetically, "Sometimes Camioneto talks too much."

Don Paco handed him a towel. Upon returning to the bedroom, he brought a shaker of talcum powder and a bottle of lotion. Luis refused the first and shook out a few drops of cologne into the palm of his hand and rubbed his face.

"No, not that way." Don Paco cupped a good amount in his left hand and began to scrub Luis's body with it. "Good after a bath. They say that toreros should smell of tobacco, wine, and women, but I like them to smell of cologne. Question of taste. Me, I'm sensitive. I like the finer things in life. Aesthetic, you might say." Now he was sprinkling the perfumed alcohol on Luis's chest, stomach, and thighs. Then he said offhandedly: "You really do have your courage well hung, don't you?"

Luis colored and turned away.

The meal was splendid. Don Paco even served them a glass of manzanilla which made Luis rather dizzy. Camioneto preferred to fill his stomach first and then drink. Two of the boys they'd seen lounging around the house waited on the table. Probably young toreros also. It seemed as though the manager guessed his thoughts.

"These kids are like my sons. They came here, like you — " he addressed himself only to Ortega — "looking for help, wanting me to feed them. They haven't moved on because they know that in exchange for very little they have everything they want."

"Don Paco — " as usual Camioneto spoke with his mouth full, "do you think the kid here can get a chance in La México?"

The man looked at Luis intensely. He pushed aside the little balls of bread his fingers had been fashioning.

"Yes, I think so. Yes, I really think so. 'Course, it depends on him — "

"That's what I tell him, Manager. That it's up to him to become a torero."

After coffee, since they were even given that, Don Paco announced that he had to leave to talk to the impresario, and he promised to bring up their names. They went out with him. While he put on his hat he motioned Luis into the office. "Don't worry about anything. I'm going to help you." He put a fatherly hand on Ortega's shoulder. "I'm going to help you, because you've got personality. I like you. You'll get some fights. But first, I want to have a talk with you. Come see me tonight at nine. Come alone —" he added, "without — you know —"

"Yes, Señor Don Paco."

As they said goodbye the manager enquired: "Need a bit of parné?"

He put two bright peso bills in Luis's hands. He rubbed the lapels of his coat with his thumbs and chewed the cigar he'd just lit.

"Don't forget. Nine o'clock!"

4

FIVE MINUTES BEFORE NINE, LUIS GOT OFF THE park bench where he'd sat since saying goodbye to Don Paco.

"Luck!" Camioneto wished him. "Didn't I tell you? Everything's going to be fine now. Don Paco took a liking to you and he's going to help you. He's a good type. Gave you the shirt you're wearing. Now you've got two. Fed you and gave you some parné. Good type, yes sir. Don Paco can work things. His toreros perform every Sunday. Take Rafaelillo. What's he got that you haven't? Nothing. When you met him he was out fighting the country wars like us, starving to death. But then he meets Don Paco and bang, he's a star overnight. What the hell's he want to see you at this hour for, though? Hell. I guess he's got his reasons. He's a little strange but you handle him right, humor him."

Luis rang. Almost instantly the door was opened. Don Paco asked him to step in. The house was silent and dimly lit. The only light was in the office. He followed the thin man. He really did smell bad. Why didn't *he* bathe and shave and use some of his cologne on himself?

"Sit down." He pointed at the sofa.

He was in his shirtsleeves with his suspenders hanging down in back. From the sideboard he brought a bottle and two glasses. He filled them. He held one out to Luis who tried to refuse it.

"Drink it. Do you good." Then he began to talk about his life in the bullfighting world, about the terrible harm women can do to toreros, about the ingrates in the fiesta brava, and a dozen other things that Luis didn't understand. Especially this: "I always make friends of my lads, my sons. Want them to love me like a father. Don't you think that's good?"

"Sure," Luis said, a little drunk now.

"I like the finer things in life. Beauty. Beautiful music, beautiful paintings, beautiful people. Beautiful relationships."

Don Paco filled his glass up again and sat down next to him. He put his glass, untouched, on the floor next to the bottle. He ran one of his hands over Luis's head.

"You have beauty in you, lad. Your eyes show you are not like your friend or the rest of these animals."

Luis frowned but didn't say anything.

"I can make you into a torero," Don Paco said quietly. "But what'll you give me in return?"

"Don Paco, you know I haven't anything. The money I make doesn't interest me that much. You keep it, if that's what you want — "

He got closer. Although he felt a little drunk Luis realized that something very strange was happening.

"Money doesn't interest me either," breathed Don Paco. "Just beauty and friendship. I'd rather have you as a friend. Money — I've got plenty for you."

"I'll earn it in the ring."

"Sure, of course. In the ring — and out of it — "

"I'm a torero."

"You're also a man, every inch a male. You and I — we'll be great friends. I'll teach you — about the different kinds of beauty. About true friendship between men. You can live here and be good to me — "

"What — how — ?"

"Just by being good to me. It's a matter you have to think about. Then, when you see how much it'll help you, it'll be easy for you."

Luis closed his eyes and threw his head back. "God, how hard that damned wine hits you!" He shook his head. If he could only get what these syrupy words of Don Paco's were driving at. Why did he want him to be good to him? How could he be? Don Paco was powerful. Then what was he asking for with his oily voice? The smell of him was getting closer to his face. All of a sudden something began to stir down there in his pants, insistent, trembling, fumbling —

Luis Ortega opened his eyes. Don Paco was struggling with a stubborn button that didn't want to come loose. He looked like a senile wild animal. He glanced up, with the look of a steer, a big, imploring steer.

Only then, finally, did Luis understand. He leapt to his feet. Don Paco flung his arms around his legs.

"Let me go!" Luis cried, frightened.

"No, no — " the man was saying.

Panicky, Luis raised his arm and he saw that his hand had

formed a fist. He let it come down heavily on Don Paco's head, once, twice, three times, again and again.

"Don't do it, don't hit me," Don Paco shrilled. "I can make you a matador, I can get you put on this Sunday's program — "

Ortega managed to free himself from his grasp. Then he kicked out and felt the point of his shoe sink deep into the man's stomach.

"Maricón de mierda," Luis spat out, "Goddamn fairy — "

He returned to the park at a run. On a bench, their bundle for a pillow, Camioneto lay smoking. Luis came up, pale and with tears in his eyes. Camioneto shook him by the shoulders.

"What happened?"

With his hands bloody and still clenched, Ortega replied: "I hit him. I broke his goddamn face for him."

"But — why?"

Luis took his time. Then he turned and Camioneto could see the tears, male and angry, on his cheeks.

"He wanted me to — to — " Luis pounded his fist into his hand. " 'I'll put you on Sunday,' he said. I hit him . . ."

Camioneto's bulldog jaw worked in fury. "Bullfighting," he said between clenched teeth, "it's stopped being a thing for men . . ."

Silent and depressed, they walked towards an avenue brightly glowing with cars and people. They were once more back where they were the night before, or worse.

5

FOR THE LAST TWO DAYS, LUIS ORTEGA HAD been able to think of nothing else but the incident with Don Paco. He felt nauseated by the whole thing. "Is this, then, the great fiesta brava?" No, it couldn't be. He imagined it as being different. Clean — with deals and intrigue, sure — but clean. He thought it was a thing of males, of real men, who risked their lives fairly and cleanly in the late sun of the afternoon. He thought that a torero's profession was a decent one, one a man wasn't ashamed of, and that the boys who stepped out into the big rings were there because they had talent in front of the horns, not in some manager's boudoir.

The following day they related the details to an ex-novillero who came into the Cantonés. They explained to him what had happened and then asked the inevitable question.

"They all like that?"

And the Blind Muñoz answered: "There are so many of them, they end up in control, and even an adding machine couldn't count up how many have to pay tribute to them!"

Now, two nights later, they were in the Tupinamba. They sat in a booth at the end near the kitchen and the urinal. It would have been better to have stayed back there, Luis thought. *Back there* was "the wars," scrounging around in country fights, full of dreams and plans, eat and sleep wherever you could, imagining beautiful things happening to you, decent, fine things. Now he regretted being in Mexico City in this center of the bullfighting world. This was all just a pile of manure wrapped prettily in silk. Yes — he should have stayed *back there*.

Conchita came over asking what their order was. They asked for two coffees with milk. They still had a few cents left from the two pesos that Don Paco had given them forty-eight hours before.

They were finishing their coffee, probably the last for several days, when suddenly there appeared before them, arms akimbo, a dark spindly youth with a basque beret and a cigarette in his mouth.

They looked at him with astonishment.

"Olé, big shots," he greeted them.

They both leapt up and embraced him unashamedly.

"Juanito Lavín! Where the hell did you crawl out of?"

They moved over in the booth to make room for him.

"We got here four days ago. Hoping to make it in La Plaza México."

"Big hopes, brother," said Juanito. "God doesn't even make it in La México without pull."

"Someone like Don Paco?"

"You've heard that already?"

"He had a run-in with him," Camioneto said.

Juanito Lavín smiled slyly at Luis.

"Did he slip it to you, boy? Don't you know that's seven years bad luck?"

Ortega blushed and shook his head.

Lavín gave them cigarettes. They lit up. They'd known him for a long time when he came bumming around Luis's home town. Since Luis already had "the bullfighting worm" eating at his insides he took him home and put him up for a while. Actually it was Juanito who first showed him how to grab a cape properly and swing a muleta. They reminisced for a while about those past times.

"And your old lady?" Juanito asked.

"She died. A year ago." Luis swallowed at the memory of the terrible death she had died. For an instant he remembered how they'd taken her to the unmarked section of the graveyard, how he'd stayed there alone, trembling and empty in his aloneness, how he had sworn that he would become the greatest matador in the world and make a million pesos and have his mother moved over to the respectable part and erect the biggest monument in the whole graveyard to her.

"I'm sorry about that," said Juanito, his good face going sad.

"She needed doctors, a hospital."

"Things only a torero can afford," said Camioneto.

"How about yours?" Luis asked.

"Dragging around as sad as usual — selling tacos in San Juan. But the old girl is still the best aficionada around. Even if it has to be the top row in the sunny section, she goes every Sunday to the fights. Not a day goes by that she doesn't tell me that if I want to be a star: 'Never take a backward step!' Sunday I'm fighting in Cuautla, and she's told me . . ."

Luis's ears pricked up. Here was a chance. He asked who was promoting it.

"Friend of mine. The Chicken."

Lavín explained that The Chicken was a cousin of the Mayor of Cuautla and it wasn't too hard for him to organize a fight in that resort town, and that he was going to appear as a matador in it.

"Do you think we could go? I mean, maybe get in a cape pass or two?"

"I'll have to talk to him."

Juanito figured that he might be able to catch him in one of the bars along the way. They crossed the street and asked for The Chicken in the Villa Madrid. He'd been there earlier —

why didn't they try the Field of Love billiard parlor? Good idea. On the way they tried the Tupinamba but they hadn't seen him there. Nor in the Flower of Mexico.

At La Chiquita they finally found The Chicken. The place was narrow and strongly impregnated with the smell of the urinal. On the walls were bullfighting pictures. Of all, Luis liked the shot of Rodolfo Gaona profiling himself before going in for the kill. There was also the mounted head of a Spanish bull, Cotorro by name, which was killed by the great Frascuelillo at the end of the last century.

"There he is," said Lavín.

He was a person of undefinable age, gaunt, dark, with a pitted face. His fingers, yellow with nicotine, pinched an incredibly short cigarette butt. He bent over to spit. With his foot he ground the phlegm into the sawdust that covered the floor. He was talking with another individual who was fat and red. They were drinking dark beer out of a pitcher.

"Chicken," Lavín interrupted.

The man twisted his fleshless face around, and a jerking motion of his head asked who wanted him.

"This is Luis Ortega and Pancho Camioneto, friends of mine — " Lavín spoke quickly as though to say the most possible in the shortest time before the man could say no. "I told them you were the impresario Sunday in Cuautla. They'd like to know if they can get in a few cape passes."

The Chicken turned around and faced them. Luis was nervous, not because he was the subject of analysis but rather because he couldn't take his eyes off the butt, which certainly was going to burn, if it hadn't already, the middle and index fingers of the novillero-impresario.

"Fought, kids?"

"Yes, in pachangas."

Lavín interceded: "Luis has a lot of class and a lot of guts. I've seen him."

"Well, you're in luck, kid." The Chicken assumed a professor's attitude as he crossed a reedy leg and chewed the nail of one thumb as he talked. " 'Cause I'm going to take you on and let you get in some passes. Nothing stingy about me."

"That's the truth," Juanito said.

"If friend Juanito here says you're good that's good enough for me. I'll put you in my cuadrilla."

Luis was getting excited. Lord, being a banderillero in a regular formal cuadrilla! Then he thought that not having a suit of lights would ruin the deal.

"The only thing is," said The Chicken after a thoughtful pause, "the gate won't stand the price of the cuadrilla's traveling expenses. If you want to fight in Cuautla you have to fix it to get there. We'll see each other on Sunday in the plaza."

"Matador," Luis said respectfully, guiltily, "the thing is, I — I don't have a real uniform."

"And what you need one for? In Cuautla it's hot as hell — " The Chicken laughed. "So we prefer to wear the corto suits. At least you've got capes, haven't you?"

"Yes."

"Then you've got everything a real torero needs. The rest is all decoration."

Luis Ortega held out his moist hand and received a long, bony, cold one in return.

"So long till Cuautla. And here's hoping it turns out fine!"

6

THEY ARRIVED AT CUAUTLA IN THE BRIGHT
sun. As they got down from the cab of the big silver oil
truck and thanked the driver profusely for the ride, he promised to come see them fight on Sunday.

"Good luck, kids."

"Thanks — thanks a thousand."

They asked where the plaza was and were directed to it:
a spindly black ring made of wood. In the town people were
still sleeping. On a corner a sign was nailed up:

BIG CORRIDA
4 FROM AGUA LIMPIA 4
FOR ANGEL SÁNCHEZ "THE CHICKEN"
    AND JUANITO LAVÍN —
TWO BULLS WILL BE KILLED —
A MUSICAL BAND AND
    BEAUTIFUL SEÑORITAS —
COMPLETE CUADRILLAS —
POPULAR PRICES

The watchman in charge of the little ring said that the bulls
would arrive the following afternoon. They asked where
they could get a bath. The best place was the river, he said.

They returned to the center of town. Camioneto said he
was hungry. "Let's scare up something for the belly."

It only took ten minutes to round out a rather respectable

menu: Camioneto came back to Luis — rather hurriedly and glancing over his shoulder — carrying in the crook of his arm, lovingly, an incredible array of groceries: fruit, bread, cheese both aged and fresh, smoked beef, tortillas, and Faro cigarettes.

"Sorry, no other brand," he apologized.

They enjoyed the naked freedom of swimming in the warm water of the river. Afterwards they spread out the cape and took a long siesta.

The following noon the bulls arrived, and they went to help with the job of unloading them into the corrals. They were four years old and ugly, with frightening horns and a wicked look about them. They were huge, larger and older (and hence smarter) than bulls you'd see in Mexico City even.

"Each one of them will go at least nine hundred pounds."

The caretaker came over to them shaking his head. He pointed to the only pinto bull, the ugliest and oldest of all.

"That berrendo is over five years old. The one just beyond him killed a man here not so long ago. It's the second one. In Jojutla he got one just last month too.

Camioneto shuddered and knocked on wood.

As they were leaving he said to Luis: "According to the bird with the hat, these bulls are so smart they know Latin. They've been fought before."

At night The Chicken and Juanito Lavín arrived by bus. They got together in the plaza. The Chicken was obviously well known in Cuautla since several passers-by said hello to him and wished him luck on Sunday.

"Seen the bulls?"

"Yes," said Luis. "They're very big."

"Did the pinto come?"

"Yes."

He shook his head. "I fought him last year and no matter how hard I tried to face-fight him he caught me and slammed me around. Now — " he turned to Lavín, "this time you get him."

"Guess it's unavoidable."

"Eaten?" The Chicken asked Luis and Camioneto.

"A little. You inviting?"

"With what? Where you sleeping?"

"In the jail. They let us sleep there."

"We're doing better in the school. I spoke to my cousin and he gave us permission. The other guys that came with us are there."

Strolling around and around the little park — "drawing water" as they called it graphically, like a well mule — they whiled away the night until eleven o'clock.

In the school where The Chicken and the others were sleeping they took possession of a vast bare room. The only decoration on the end wall was a portrait of Benito Juárez, mounted on colored crepe paper. Someone took out a candle end, lit it and placed it in the center of the room. Capes and muletas were thrown on the dusty floor and the toreros stretched out on them.

The Chicken amused himself by rolling a huge cigarette. Luis watched him by the flickering candlelight. It was a strange looking thing. It wasn't a cigar or a plain cigarette either. The Chicken finished rolling it, licked it, and pinched the ends. His companions didn't take their eyes off it.

As The Chicken lit his cigarette from it, the candle almost went out. As he inhaled the smoke he let out a penetrating and sibilant sound. He held the smoke in a long time before blowing it out.

"Pass it over," muttered the torero next to him.

The Chicken took one more long drag and then passed it

on. He inhaled twice and handed it to the next. And so it came around to Luis.

"What is it?" Luis asked cautiously.

The other boy looked at him, surprised. "The weed, the happy weed. Don't you want it?"

"No."

"And you guys?" he asked Camioneto and Juanito Lavín.

"Us neither. We don't use it."

Then he passed the cigarette on after taking another puff. It smelled rancid, like burning straw. Luis felt that his eyes were falling out with sleepiness. He wrapped himself up in the muleta and rolled over.

A few minutes later, half asleep, he barely heard the others getting gay and giggly.

7

CAMIONETO HADN'T BEEN WRONG WHEN HE had pronounced judgment on the bulls the day before. They really did "know Latin." The pinto handed Juanito Lavín a terrible tossing. When the bull was finally herded out, everyone breathed easier. Then began what was called the formal part of the fight, the fight to the death of the other pair of treacherous beasts. Sweating blood, The Chicken finally managed to dispatch the bull he'd drawn. Juanito had a bad time with his on the cape, and then to please the crowd, already very drunk and noisy, he decided to place the banderillas himself. The bull was so tricky and wise to the ways of man that he was only able to get one of the sticks of the first pair in and of the second pair one ended up not far from the animal's tail and the other down on its neck.

But the crowd wanted to see more. He came over to the fence for another pair.

"It's hooking badly to the right on you," Luis warned.

For a second Juanito looked at him, telling him with his eyes of the fear that was enveloping him. The bull was dangerous on both sides, jerking his head in the middle of a pass, hooking frightfully at the men, charging with its feet first instead of putting its head down and charging honestly.

Licking his fingers and then moistening the barbed points of the banderillas, Juanito asked The Chicken to flash a cape from behind the fence and attract its attention. Then, running fast, Juanito started his trip in towards the bull. The bull whirled and charged hard for him. Luis saw that something was going to happen, because the bull was too tricky to charge straight, but rather headed off to the side, leading the man the way a hunter leads a bird with his shotgun blast. When they came together there was nothing to be done, no escape. The wicked head slashed violently to the right and there was a sound like breaking bones. Juanito Lavín, like a rag doll, went hurtling up into the air to fall head first and unconscious to the hard sand.

They all ran to lure the bull away, but the animal paid no attention to them and vented its fury on the inert body of the young torero. When Luis saw that shouts and flashing of capes in its face did no good he grabbed one horn and the tail of the animal, and jerked on them fiercely, and it finally swung away from its victim and chased Luis. Luis almost got tossed himself as he lured the bull to another part of the ring. The drunken crowd let out delighted guffaws.

They picked up Juanito and rushed him away. The Chicken felt him all over and declared he wasn't hurt, that it was just a blow, not a goring. They laid him safely behind a wooden burladero shield. The fight had been interrupted and now the crowd howled for some action.

Trembling and green, The Chicken, as the senior matador, had to take up the sword and muleta now and try to dispatch the animal. Ortega saw in his face unspeakable panic. The man's lips had gone chalky white.

"Head way off to the side," rasped another torero, "and let him have it in the lungs!"

"All right," The Chicken stammered.

That wasn't the way to do it, Luis thought. It'd be much better to act decisively with this animal, show it who was master and go right straight in at it, nothing else. "Never a backward step," Juanito's mother used to say. Luis suddenly said to himself, The Chicken may be afraid, but I'm not. The Chicken was hanging back along the fence now, the muleta and sword uselessly at his side. The bull, out in the center, was shaking its head in the clear hot air, wagging its horns defiantly.

"Now!"

Luis ran up to The Chicken and snatched the cape and sword from his hands. Surprised, The Chicken offered no resistance. He watched this young boy, skinny and determined, as he ran out towards the bull. And he saw the boy slip down to his knees three yards away from the bull, shaking the red muleta rag and shouting at it.

"Look out," The Chicken shouted, "it's going to get you!"

Never had a bull's head seemed bigger or more ferocious to Luis. But Christ almighty, toreros weren't made to die in childbirth!

Luis was thinking: the reason this animal has been in command is that no one has had the guts to "cross" with it properly, to work very close to it and never step back. He began moving forward, forward, *across* the line of its intended charge, not *away* from it the way the others had done. It looked as though it were about to charge.

"Toro, ah-hah!"

The pounding sound became louder than the clamor of the crowd, and it was the impossibly loud beating of his heart. Then the earth under his knees began to shake suddenly.

He didn't know whether he'd closed his eyes, only that all of a sudden he saw that the horns had gone past him. Brushing past him, as long as a freight train, was the black muscular bulk of the beast. He inched forward again on his knees as the bull wheeled.

"Toro, toma!" he shouted, this time with more confidence. He let the bull come by closer this time. There followed four more passes, each closer to the animal than the one before it. When he got to his feet he felt drunk, not the way he'd felt from Don Paco's alcohol but in a completely different and marvelous way.

As he continued fighting, he saw nothing, he heard nothing, he felt nothing apart from the bull, the enormous thrill of fighting a bull beautifully. They were moments of complete insanity, of sacrifice, of offering his hungry flesh to the executioner-horn that scraped his belly, slashing past his thighs.

Then with his vision clouded, with his body feeling like a slab of lead, he raised the sword and hurled himself into the blackness. Luis Ortega felt himself flying, flung away from the earth up into the air like a fragile reed. The arena spun before his eyes, comically upside down.

And a great long cry went up:

"Oooooléee," gigantic, unending, eternal.

When he began to come to and understand what **was going** on he found himself running around the ring, his face bloody and teary, the ears and the tail of the bull in his hands.

While he took lap after wonderful, delirious lap, his companions followed him, catching in the stretched out cape the coins that were flung down to him from the stands.

Among all the faces, Luis spotted one that he recognized — the truck driver who had brought them to Cuautla. Luis stopped a moment and threw up one of the ears that had been awarded him. The recipient gestured a slap on the back in gratitude.

"Torero! Torero!" The coveted chant with which the crowd rewards a triumphant matador cracked down from the stands. It was a beautiful sound, the most beautiful Luis Ortega had ever heard in his scant eighteen years.

Afterwards they went down to the river to swim and that night they went to the little restaurant for dinner. The Chicken spilled out the money they'd collected in the ring onto the clothless table. There were thirty-two pesos, and forty centavos. They divided it up into equal parts, and then fell to talking about toreros and bulls and bullfighting and the great performances of history.

8

IT HAD BEEN RAINING IN THE CITY SINCE early afternoon. The streets were empty and as gray as death. Ortega and Camioneto had spent their last cent, all that was left from Cuautla, on coffee and buns. As they handed the money over to the waitress in the Cantonés, they felt as though they were losing the last proof of that great triumph.

"Once again," Luis sighed, "no parné."

"Once again like always," Camioneto corrected him.

They stayed there, talking, dreaming, or lapsing into long silences until Conchita came up and told them to get out because Pepe, the Chinaman, was going to close up. They went out into the street, hands in their pockets, caps pulled down to their eyes, the bundle under an arm. The Tupinamba, the Do Brasil, the elegant cafés of Bolívar Street, had their doors locked already.

It would soon be two o'clock. Where to go? The Garden of the Frog was, as usual, drenched. In the doorways, the newspaper sellers and the bums had all the dry spots staked out. Just to be doing something they walked. It must have been very late when they reached a spot out of which music was coming. They lifted their eyes to read, through the curtain of drizzle, the letters of green neon:

The Cricket Cabaret

"Let's take a leak," Camioneto suggested.

They went in. It was hot and smoky. In amongst the low lights they could see men and women of strange hues. An orchestra of mulattos played something tropical. A woman brushed by Luis, bumping him with her round and gelatinous buttocks, and he tried to think how long it had been since he'd gone to bed with a girl. "Uy! As my mother used to say," he said with a smile. This business of having a woman was a problem for a beginning torero like himself, a real problem. There was always the other business, but they said that was bad for your health. The first days the desire was always there, nagging at you. Then it shut up and left you alone for a while. Camioneto always watched him like a father and tried to keep him away from women and those who talked about them too much. "You're never going to get anything out of one of those heifers — " were his words, "except a good healthy dose." And then he launched into a discourse about the evil that whores cause to the blood and spirit of those who wish to don a suit of lights with dignity.

"Let's go." Camioneto whistled as he came out of the toilet buttoning his fly.

"Wait a minute," Luis said. "It's raining outside. At least it's warm here."

"We'll find a place to sleep — come on." He tugged at his sleeve.

A girl, blond and very painted, came up. Her gum snapped as she chewed. She stood in front of them and cocked her head in a way that was appealing to Luis.

"Hola," she said.

"Hola," Ortega repeated.

"What are you drinking? Want me to join you?"

He shook his head, confused. As always, when in trouble, Luis's hands began to sweat and he stammered: "We're — we're just leaving."

"Why so soon?" The girl had slipped her arm through his.

"We just came in to — to use the toilet," said the torero. "Leaving now."

She laughed, without missing a beat of her gum-chewing.

"You look scared. I don't eat people — "

Camioneto drew himself up. "Luis isn't afraid of anyone, much less a *buñí* like you."

Now the girl faced Camioneto. "What kind of language are you talking? What the hell's a buñí?"

"What you are, baby, a — a"

"A tramp?"

"Yes."

"Hah," the girl said. "And so what? Afraid of me?"

Luis lowered his eyes, without answering. His mouth

tasted bitter, as when he knelt down in front of that bull in Cuautla. He couldn't understand why he'd been able to stand up to that lousy bull and now he was giving down to this washed-out little blonde, who'd taken him by the arm.

"Yes," he managed, hoarsely.

The blonde let out a laugh. This amused her. Because of the rain there weren't many men around and she could talk to these boys, even though they weren't drinking anything. She led Luis off to a darkened corner. Camioneto limped behind not liking anything about it.

"What's your name?" she said, offering him a cigarette, which he didn't take.

"Luis — Luis Ortega."

"Me, I'm Estela. Do you work or — " She broke off the sentence to light her cigarette. ". . . or what?"

Through the smoke she studied the timid boy in front of her: He's just a kid. A little bigger than she, but still a child. She could see that he had beautiful eyes and she guessed that in daylight his brown hair would look even lighter. His friend, though, was unpleasant and ugly.

Camioneto cut in: "What do you think he does! He's a torero."

"Torero?" Estela opened her eyes wide and her mouth opened. "Torero! And here I always thought they'd — be different."

"How?" Luis said, a little offended. "What you think they'd be like?"

"Just — different, that's all. Waltz around in their sequins, and so forth. So you're a torero. Honest?"

"Yes."

"Where do you live?" she asked abruptly.

"No place. Haven't any parné for bunking."

"Hey, talk so I can understand you."

"The matador here just means that we got no money for a hotel," Camioneto translated.

"What are you going to do then?"

"When the water quits coming down we'll look for a place to flop. And if it doesn't quit, we'll just walk around. Won't be the first night."

It was getting better all the time. So they were toreros! It seemed unbelievable that these ragged and chilled kids who admitted they didn't even have a place to spend the night could be toreros. And just to think how she had always yearned to meet one, to see one up close! An idea came to her. She put her hands with their painted nails on Luis's. She looked at him deeply amidst the shadowy smell of smoke and of stale armpits and urinals.

"I live in a hotel, nearby," she explained. Her breath was faintly alcoholic, no matter how she tried to cover up with mint gum. "If you want to wait for me when I'm through I'll take you up there."

"We haven't any money," Ortega said.

She stood up. "What's it matter?" She gave a gay laugh. "I'm not going to charge toreros."

And she walked away, swinging her stern under the shiny satin. Involuntarily, Luis's eyes caressed the flesh that jiggled with the woman's every step, and he felt a surge in his loins, as though it were another heart beating down there.

Camioneto watched him. He knew Luis better than anyone and he caught the flash in his eyes. For a long minute no one spoke. Then Ortega heard Camioneto say:

"You're thinking things, aren't you?"

"What are you talking about?"

"You're thinking of doing it with her." Luis was going to deny it, but he lowered his eyes. "Don't bother to talk," said Camioneto. "Let's go."

"Wait." The word came out like a hammer blow. It was said in a hard dry tone Luis never used in speaking.

Camioneto obeyed, surprised.

"We're going to wait," said Luis.

Almost at five, Estela poked his shoulder. Both were dozing face forward on the table. She was wearing a black plastic raincoat. She was cinching up the belt.

"Ready! Let's get a move on."

The bed was wide, of iron painted white. One didn't have to be too bright to guess that it hadn't been made very often. The mattress and sheets were in complete disarray. Estela turned on a lamp, and took off her raincoat and shoes. Ortega and Camioneto, immobile, embarrassed, watched her.

Turning around she said: "What you waiting for? Jump in."

Camioneto untied the bundle and spread the cape and muleta out on the floor. As he did, he explained to the girl, who had shed her dress and was now in her slip: "All toreros always sleep on the floor — helps stay in shape." Luis never took his eyes off the hard nipples which were straining against Estela's rayon slip.

"Listen," she said to Luis, "all three of us won't fit in the bed, so you come."

He declined, shaking his head. "Thanks, I'm used to the boards."

"You a fairy, that it? Nothing's going to happen to you, baby."

Luis glanced over at Camioneto. If he'd only say all right! Camioneto's eyes were fishlike and noncommittal. He shrugged his shoulders and pulled the cape over him, over his head even.

Slowly, Luis Ortega took off his shirt. Estela, sitting on the bed, watched him unabashedly. He was going to undo the sash that acted as a belt to hold up his pants, but he hesitated.

"Turn out the light."

Camioneto, from his burrow in the capes, heard a little laugh. He chewed a curse around in his mouth but didn't let it out. Estela turned out the light. The bed squeaked as Luis stretched out on it. Many minutes later, the man sleeping on the floor gathered that for those in bed, the evening had just begun.

9

IT WAS THE SECOND TIME IN FIFTEEN DAYS that Luis Ortega had quit from fatigue after half an hour of working out.

"That's enough, Camioneto," he was gasping for breath. He leaned up against the barrera fence and shook his head as though to get rid of a weight that was pressing on the lower part of his skull. He had suddenly gone white. I'm a little done in. Let's go . . ."

Camioneto spat and ground the saliva with his foot. His face was an angry red as he snapped the cape into folds and jerked the four corners of the bundle together.

Without speaking they walked towards Insurgentes Avenue. On the corner they waited for a bus.

"You're through, Luis."

"What's the matter with you?"

"That's what I want to know — what's the matter with you?"

"Can't somebody get a little tired working out?"

"You didn't used to talk like that. You used to be the first one to want to get out and start working. 'Course, that was before."

"Spit it out."

"Ever since you met Estela, you're like you been castrated — but really — just like a castrated bull."

"Don't start on her," Luis turned, threateningly.

"Get's you, doesn't it? It's her fault. Every night, every goddamn night, you're leaving any talent you might have in her."

"That's not so." But Luis knew it was. He was *manso* — tame — weak, with his legs shaky and a lassitude throughout his whole body that he couldn't shake. She never got tired.

"It wasn't so long ago," Camioneto said, "you were knocking Rafaelillo for thinking more about the buñís than the bulls. Now what about you?"

"Anyway, stay out of it."

The red bus pulled up and they got on.

10

AFTER THE TURKISH BATH THEY DROPPED BY the café. When they got back, Estela was still sleeping, naked. When Luis covered her up she opened her eyes and asked what time it was. Twelve o'clock. She grunted that she was really hung over and asked him to bring her a beer. When Luis went out, Camioneto said to the girl: "Why don't you let him go?"

"Let him — when we go so well together? Hah!"

"If you love him, leave him. You're sucking him dry like a lemon. He's just skin and bones."

Estela sat up in bed. She moaned that her head ached. She leaned over to spit, not caring whether Camioneto saw the breasts hanging from her dark body. When she leaned back she retorted: "Really? And wasn't he worse off before? Skinny and weak. Isn't it thanks to me that he's got money and food? And don't you too? Just by the way?"

"Sure — but before he was skinny from hunger — not because of some buñí."

"You lousy —"

Luis came in. He had three bottles. He opened them and left them on the dresser. He said he and Camioneto were going to the café and that he'd be back later in the afternoon. Estela, after a few pulls on one of the bottles, lay back on the bed. She belched.

As they went out into the street, Luis asked, "What was going on in there?"

"Nothing. I was just saying she ought to let you alone."

"And what right you got to stick your nose into this?"

"I'll tell you what right — the right of a friend — somebody who's gone hungry and suffered with you, that's what right! Somebody who doesn't want to see them leave you crazy with a dose in your blood that even Doctor Rojo de la Vega couldn't cure!" Camioneto had to stop for breath before going on. "Don't forget one thing, boy, the bulls you're going to have to take on will always be four years old — always — and young and strong — and you, every year you'll be older and less in shape. You're not going any place, Luis Ortega, if you keep leaving all your energy with a buñí every night!"

Since he'd met Estela and received a five-peso bill from her every morning, Luis hadn't stepped inside the Café Cantonés once. He had changed physically and mentally. He dressed now almost nattily, and instead of secondhand sneakers he sported real leather shoes. He wasn't thinking about how a torero has to go hungry and have lots of *afición*. He was thinking that life is made to be lived and that nothing could compare with a little easy money and some hot soup. And best of all a woman whenever you felt like it, arms around you, legs around you — not love but a substitute, better than nothing, much better than the aloneness, the womanlessness of his existence this past year.

He liked to go to the Tupinamba and to occupy a table near the big window that looked out to Bolívar Street so he could see the people and they could see him. And that's where they sat now and rather elegantly ordered some food.

They were on the fourth cup of coffee when The Chicken arrived. He leaned over Luis.

"Been tracking you all morning. Even went to the hotel. Your woman said you were in the Tupi."

He wasn't sure he liked her being called his woman. He was a little ashamed of her.

"What's the action?"

The Chicken hunched his shoulders forward. He took a cigarette that Luis offered.

"Good action. Got a friend who's getting a fight together Sunday in Jojutla. I'm on, and I thought you'd like to go too."

Camioneto moved his chair over next to The Chicken's.

"And how about the parné?"

"Not much. It could cover your expenses though. Coming?"

"Course we're coming," said Camioneto.

"When do we have to be there?" Luis asked.

"Up to you. The pachanga is on Sunday."

Thursday Estela didn't come home to sleep. Luis waited until four, when she generally came back from The Cricket. At nine, he went sleepily to the plaza with Camioneto. When they came back, the girl was just going upstairs smelling of the heat and sex. She babbled into Luis's face with her bad breath.

"I'm leaving tonight," he announced simply.

Estela went in and undressed in front of the two men.

"Where for?" She got her eyes, which were suffering from a tendency to cross now, to focus blearily on Luis.

"To Jojutla, to fight."

"Won't let you. Don't want you to go."

A fight was building and Camioneto decided to pull out and leave them alone. Estela clung to Luis's neck. He pried her arms loose. With his back to her he tried to make his voice hard and manly.

"I'm going, I said, so shut up unless you want some chipped teeth."

"Why you going? Something could happen to you," she moaned pathetically. She began to cry, "Bull could hurt you. Don't want you to be a torero. Don't have to be — you know everything I make is yours . . ."

"I said I was going."

"Well, tell them you aren't." Her slender body writhed. "If you want, I won't go out at night and we'll just stay here, you and me."

Although he had to keep his word with The Chicken, the idea didn't appeal much to Luis. For the first time in his eighteen years, he had known what comfortable easy living was, living without scrounging for a lousy hunk of bread for one's belly. This woman represented a peaceful existence, without the terrible fear of risking one's neck against a vicious beast in some nameless arena. Maybe she was right! She'd talked about how he could get hurt. Why did he have to go out looking for danger anyway, when here in this room he had everything he needed — everything, money and pleasure, just for the asking? The Chicken would know how to handle the affair without him. There were plenty of maniacs around who just for the pleasure of making a cape pass or two would go not only to Cuautla or Jojutla but to the end of the world. He'd see him in the café that night and tell him he was sick and to chase up someone else.

And Camioneto? What would he say? What excuse could he get him to swallow. Camioneto was too smart — he'd know right away that the reason Luis wasn't going was because he lacked guts, because he was *manso*, because he was afraid. "Damn Camioneto!"

Estela was waiting for an answer. Luis looked hard at her.

"I've got to go. I gave my word."

She drew back like a cat. Her hair fell over her unwashed and streaked face. Her lips drew back to rasp:

"If you go, you don't get back. I give you whatever you want to keep you here. Been supporting you, and I got rights. If you go, get this straight — don't come back — "

Luis went out, slamming the door.

11

THE FIGHT IN JOJUTLA WAS VERY BAD.

"Keep your feet still, you goddamn fairy!" This sentence, shouted all afternoon by Camioneto, stung Luis Ortega like a quirt lash across the face. But he couldn't stand up to that bull. When he saw it charging, he felt his legs go rubbery felt his stomach go hollow, and then he'd run, run like a scared child from the bogeyman.

The agony was drawn out beyond eternity, and Luis Ortega suffered the humiliation of having a rancher shout out from the stands that he was a castrated steer, that he was without guts, to fight this bull so badly, a bull which, incidentally, he was unable to kill.

After the fight The Chicken told him not to take it too much to heart, to remember that anybody could have a bad day and that the best thing to do was to have a drink or two. From his knapsack he took out a bottle of mezcal and offered it to Luis, who took a long pull from it.

"I been thinking of a good deal," The Chicken was saying.

Luis wasn't listening. Ever since he'd left Mexico City in that second class bus, he'd been thinking of nothing but Estela and her threat. "If you go — don't come back." He was sure that her anger would have blown over by now and that when she saw him, things would be like before. And supposing not? What was going to happen if she didn't. Only one answer: Back to hunger and sleeping wherever one could. I shouldn't have come, he kept saying to himself. Hard to believe, but one's faculties can really go to hell. And what happened: the bull had taken over and damned near killed him.

"What do you think, Luis?" The Chicken must be talking to him.

"Of what," he said, "of what?"

"I was just saying, that the best thing would be to keep fighting around here. As you've seen, these people really go in for the bulls and we should go on to other towns. 'Course, I can't do it alone — need you to come."

Luis declined.

"No, Chicken, I'm going back. I don't want to even smell

a bull around these parts. Now, if you want to talk about a fight in La México . . ."

Camioneto glanced at him with his sideways look. He shook his head, spat and stood up.

"This one's a dead pigeon, Chicken," he said. "That buñí in Mexico City killed off any afición he had. Drop him. Find yourself another, a man, but a real man . . ."

Luis's face went white with blind fury. With a leap he was on his feet. Suddenly his hand was bristling with a puntilla knife. He flung himself on Camioneto and the two of them struggled in a convulsive lock. Then Camioneto managed to kick the knife out of Luis's hands. Camioneto flung himself on him then and slammed his fist again and again into the other's face until he could swing no more.

"Leave him, you've given him enough," The Chicken said.

Camioneto got up, panting and wet with sweat. He picked up the puntilla, looked at it with scorn, and flung it beside Luis, who still lay on the ground, his face bruised and broken.

Camioneto took the bundle and signaled to The Chicken.

"Let's go, it stinks around here."

12

FOR MORE THAN AN HOUR LUIS PACED AROUND in front of the hotel, without being able to make up his mind to go in. One thought still filled his brain: that Estela wouldn't take him back. The terrible thing was that he needed this buñí — needed her terribly, worse than he needed bullfighting and the things that it promised. Weak! he accused himself. Weak! He gave a last drag on his cigarette, spat, and went into the darkened hall whose darkness was only slightly relieved by a pale orange light bulb.

It must be past three and she'd be asleep now. He went up the stairs slowly. Still on his face, lividly, were Camioneto's punches. Yet it didn't seem right without him. He turned the handle of the door and went into the room. He looked first at the bed. Estela, naked, was taking off her shoes.

Her mouth widened in a sneer. "So you came back."

"You see me," he muttered, "don't you?"

"And Camioneto?"

"He didn't come."

"Why not?"

"He didn't come, that's all."

A silence. Luis slung his cap into a corner and took off his shirt. He poured some water in the basin and began to wash his bruised face. The rest of his body was also decorated here and there with bruised splotches under the skin, an eloquent résumé of his fights with the bull. His back ached and near his right armpit there was a violet shadow.

"How'd it go?" he heard her ask.

"Bad," he answered, his face in the towel, and with an attempt at nonchalance.

He hung it up on the nail next to the mirror on the wall, and turned to Estela. Arms around her knees, she hadn't moved. Luis sitting on the edge of the bed, shed his shoes and pants. The girl whistled when she saw the bruises on his naked body.

"Really rough?"

He nodded. He got in between the sheets, his back to her. He didn't want her to see the angry tears which had suddenly sprung to his eyes. Every one of those bruises was an accusation, a taunting reproach, an echo of Camioneto's voice. Other times he'd taken a beating from the bulls, sure, but *fighting*, trying. This time it was different: that bastard of a bull had given it to him simply because Luis was too short to get away from it.

Estela's warm fingers caressed his back, which smelled of stale sweat. They went up to his neck and tickled his ears. Then he felt her breath as she kissed the nape of his neck.

He felt himself set aflame, as usual. Luis knew what had to come now. But he wasn't going to allow it. He was broken inside and outside, too exhausted to make love. And hurting badly all over.

"I'll cure you," Estela murmured, hunching her body tight up against Luis's.

He sat up, leaning on an elbow. His voice suddenly was an angry whiplash.

"For Christ's sake relax! I don't feel like it!"

"Well don't yell at me!"

"Shut up!"

Estela saw such savagery in his face that she obeyed and lay back.

13

THE BOY WHO SAID HIS NAME WAS RAFAEL Rodríguez, from Aguascalientes, showed up in the Cantoné and dragged a chair over to the table where the gang was.

Juanito Lavín offered him a cigarette and then asked how things were going.

"Soon, soon," he answered.

"Seen the impresario?"

"Yes. Said he was going to give me a chance soon."

"You got to stay on top of them, the lousy beggars."

"And Luis?" Rafael asked Pancho Camioneto. Camioneto looked at him a moment, removing the ash from his Delicado with his little finger.

"I don't know," he said indifferently. "Haven't seen him for a long time."

Gallego Alvárez, another boy who wanted to be a torero, spoke up, his gold teeth flashing: "Pancho dumped him. He's a loco."

"He sure is," said someone else.

Camioneto bristled.

"Luis Ortega is no loco, nor a bum like us. This type — this type has the makings of a great torero. The day they put him on in La México he's going to bring the house down like nobody you ever saw."

"Then how come he isn't with you anymore?"

"We had a little argument, that's all. The bastard's wandering around with a sword sticking out of his withers like a bull — a sword thrust handed him by a buñí. When he gets out of heat he'll get up there where he belongs. The day this boy makes up his mind, he'll be the greatest torero in the world, you'll see!"

Artist Morales who had been silent up to now spoke up to say he didn't agree.

"The women," he said emphatically, "they're death for a torero. Look at me. I could have been a star, because I had everything — class, the build, guts, but I fell in love with a buñí, Esperanza was her name — used to work in La Chiquita — still does, matter of fact. For years I spent my money on her. My youth disappeared and the great torero that could have been became transformed into a clown. That's right, a big clown whose half-verónica in the door of a saloon and whose afaroladas on a car or a bus going down this street have never been equaled or ever will be — "

When Luis Ortega walked in, all their heads turned towards the door. He was dressed in a chamois skin jacket, gabardine pants, and elk skin shoes. A cigarette hung from his lips.

Juanito nudged Camioneto: "Look, the bastard's left his pals at the Tupi and has stooped to coming back amongst the poor people."

Uncertainly, like the first night, Luis hung back at the door. He saw the gang way in the back and started for them. His shoes squeaked and someone made a remark. Under other circumstances Luis might have looked for a fight. Now he pretended he hadn't heard anything. Since the Jojutla incident, two weeks had gone by, two weeks of steady partying in Estela's room. The fact was, this was the first night he'd left the hotel. Things, for some mysterious reason, seemed different, and so did the people. The world has changed, he said to himself. What brought him to the Cantonés? He couldn't explain, just as he couldn't explain a lot of things. But here he was. He could have gone to the Tupinamba, the Do Brasil, the Flower of Mexico. He had enough money. Perhaps, although he tried to put it out of his mind, perhaps it was because here he might bump into Camioneto.

The eyes of the youths at the table kept boring into him as he came closer. He could see different expressions in their faces: some mocking, some disdainful, the others indifferent.

"Hola," he addressed them in general.

"Hola," replied Rodríguez, in the same tone.

"How goes everything?"

"Fine."

A silence descended. From the street came the night noises of the city. A hurdy-gurdy cranked out the ranchera melody "Two Little Trees." A streetcar clanged by. An auto horn insulted another car sharply.

"Pancho," said Luis, breaking the silence, which was full of unsaid words. "Pancho — let's go eat. I got some parné on me."

The invitation was for Camioneto exclusively. Everyone's gaze swung from Luis to look at Camioneto. Again the din of silence, full of tension.

Camioneto raised his face. Luis couldn't read even a hope in it. It was a frozen, expressionless mask.

"Let's go," he said, "it stinks around here." Everyone in the group stood up.

Juanito Lavín was the only one who, as he passed, pressed his hand on Luis's arm briefly. That touch, and the feeling that he wasn't completely alone, Luis Ortega would never forget.

When they'd all gone and he stayed there as rigid as a statue, Luis once again felt hot tears of fury and aloneness in his eyes.

14

THREE TIMES THERE WAS A KNOCK AT THE door. Estela grunted for him to go see who it was.

Who the hell? Luis thought as he lurched to his feet. He focused his sleep-filled eyes with difficulty on the wrist watch Estela had given him a few days ago. The hands indicated that it was eleven-thirty. He had to lean against the bed to keep from falling. Tequila fumes were still numbing his brain. His foot knocked over a bottle of liquor on the floor and it rolled across the floor to bang against the wall.

"Christ, you're still half bombed," mumbled the girl.

Yes, he was, and if there was any doubt about it his head would remind him, since it seemed to be a separate entity, independent of his body and miles from his feet.

Stumbling over to the door, he opened it.

"Hola, Matador!"

It was Rafaelillo who greeted him so cheerfully.

"What you want?"

"I've come to invite you."

"Where to?"

"Where you can make yourself some pesos."

"What cockeyed scheme you got now?"

"No scheme. Let's swing a cape or two over at La México."

Luis shook his head and when he did it felt as though it were going to split. He pressed his fingers against his eyeballs to lessen the pain.

"Get somebody else. I'm sick."

"You're hung, which is something else again. Well, whatever you say. But I was going to slip you a loan and introduce you to somebody — " This just came to Rafaelillo as he went along to whet Luis's interest he had thought of him because he knew that he was capable of doing anything for money. Smiling, he awaited his answer. "Coming or not?"

Why not go? Although Luis felt terrible, as though his stomach was going to flip completely over, a little exercise in some fresh air might do him some good. Might sweat out some of the alcohol and get in some kind of shape to face the rest of the day.

Rafaelillo stepped in the room, sniffing. It smelled of

everything, of woman, sex, and drink. He looked at Estela, who was snoring now with her mouth open, spit dribbling on the pillow.

"That your woman?"

"Yes," Luis admitted, ashamed.

"Bet you're really getting a workout too."

Luis got into his pants heavily and knotted the shirt. He grabbed his cap and motioned to Rafaelillo to slip out quietly. As he closed the door behind them, Luis asked: "Who you going to introduce me to?"

"To the impresario. He's going to be there at twelve."

On the way, as he drove fast down Insurgentes, Rafael told Luis how he was going to be on this Sunday, along with Joselillo and Fernando López, and that Don Paco had used his pull to get him into the Corrida of the Press, which would be a really important fight in his career.

"Don't like to boast," said Rafaelillo, "but if I feel like it, you're going to see me just finish those other bums once and for all."

As they were going down the ramp to the cuadrilla gate, they passed Camioneto and Juanito Lavín who had just finished working out. Juanito waved briefly as they passed. Pancho looked through him.

"Have a fight?" Rafaelillo asked.

"Something like that," Luis mumbled.

For half an hour, Luis acted as the bull for Rafael to practice with. Then the novillero said he'd worked out enough and told Luis to fold up the capes and muleta, while he went over to say hello to a man in a gray suit, whom he treated very respectfully.

Luis sagged down on the stirrup board and waited for Rafael to finish his interview. Finally, he motioned Luis to come over.

"Doctor," Rafaelillo took the impresario by the arm, "this is Luis Ortega. Friend of mine and a good torero."

"How do you do," said Luis, coloring, and held out his hand to the almighty.

The impresario smiled without taking the hand. As they walked up the tunnel towards where they left his car, Rafaelillo said: "If you can, give him some help."

The impresario turned. "Luis Ortega, eh? Come see me one of these days in my office."

"Yes, sir," Luis stammered.

As they were heading back to the city, Rafaelillo snapped open the Cadillac's glove compartment and took out a flask of brandy. He took a drink and offered one to Luis.

"It's Fundador. Nothing better after a workout."

He invited Luis to join him in a Turkish bath at the Regis. Luis felt very out of place in that elegant place where everyone greeted his companion and wished him luck. While they sweated in the steam room, Rafaelillo kept pulling on the flask of Fundador and advised Luis.

"Look, Luis, don't be a fool. Do what I told you. Don Paco — " he winked one eye — "he's forgotten what happened and he's willing to give you another chance. Don't miss it again. You'll see how he can really fix you up like nobody else. There were twenty dying to get on this Sunday and yet look who made it — me."

Luis could only mumble: "Maybe you're right."

Once again outside in the street under a blazing sun, they said goodbye. As he'd promised, Rafaelillo gave him five pesos.

"Remember now," he said, "I'll expect you on Sunday in the hotel to help me get dressed."

Slowly, as though someone else were operating his legs, Luis crossed through the green island of freshness that is the

Alameda. He crossed Juárez, went up Madero, and headed for the café.

15

RAFAELILLO WAS JUST GETTING OUT OF HIS bath when they rang at his door. With his chin he signaled for Luis to open it.

"Congratulations!" greeted a voice.

Rafaelillo had sat down on the bed, after taking off the elegant robe of red silk. From the bureau he took a bottle of cologne and began to rub his body.

"What's up, Manager?"

It was Don Paco who came in, as skinny and slow as ever, and still chewing on an unlighted cigar. With the butt of his cane he poked Luis lightly in the stomach. He smiled and shoved his homburg back with his thumb. Luis felt himself pale in front of this man whom he'd struck that terrible evening. But Don Paco seemed to remember nothing and went on with friendly smoothness.

"Hola," he said to Luis. "Hola, big boy."

Silently, Luis began to attach Rafaelillo's artificial pigtail. The matador, closely shaved and reeking of cologne, lit a cigarette. With his head cocked to keep the smoke out of his eyes, he asked: "How are the bulls, Don Paco?"

Don Paco replied, with his chin resting on the head of the cane: "Strong. But with comfortable heads."

"Ah! And Joselillo's?"

"Good. He always has luck in the drawing."

Other friends drifted in. The process of dressing the matador proceeded slowly. Through the window opening out into the Paseo de la Reforma came the humid aroma of the trees and the far-off drone of cars. A balloon vender's whistle split the air periodically to tell the children he was around; it was a long, thin sound, as sharp as a Toledo blade.

Ortega, kneeling, was adjusting the matador's knee tassels. He felt Don Paco's gaze boring into him, so he didn't raise his head.

"And you?" he heard himself asked, "what have you been up to?"

Since Luis didn't answer right away Rafaelillo answered for him: "Still dying to fight bulls. But — " he winked an eye at the manager — "he still hasn't made up his mind."

"That true?" Don Paco poked him on the shoulder with his cane.

Luis preferred not to answer.

"And just why don't you want to be a friend of mine?" Don Paco went on. "I can make you a star, as I've done for so many. Put you on Sunday after Sunday, and for good money. Rafaelillo here will tell you whether or not I'm lying."

Someone knocked at the door. Before being told Luis ran to see who it was. He opened the door a bit and saw through the crack a woman wearing a silver fox cape.

"Rafael here?" she asked, on tiptoes trying to see into the room over Luis's shoulder.

"Yes, dressing."

"I've come to see him."

"I don't — he's getting dressed."

"I know, I know," said the girl impatiently. "Let me in."

"I better ask."

"Tell him it's Aurora."

Don Paco had come over to find out what the fuss was

about. Luis felt the manager put a hand on his shoulder, and he turned away, brusquely.

"What's your problem?"

"I want to see Rafaelillo. I'm his fiancée."

"See him in the arena."

"But I'm his fiancée — " It was her only weapon.

Don Paco gave his cigar a dry bite. Hardly moving his lips he said: "Beat it, baby. If you want to see him buy yourself a ticket."

He slammed the door. They could hear Aurora ranting outside and then her high heels beating a furious tattoo down the hall.

"Who was it?" Rafael wanted to know.

Don Paco stood in front of him, the cane in both hands.

"Some bitch who wanted to wish you luck."

"What she look like?"

Luis said, "She said her name was Aurora."

"Ah!"

The cigar was transferred from one side of his mouth over to the other and when Don Paco spoke he showed his yellow, uneven teeth.

"Still messing around with that?"

Rafael turned and retorted, "Yes, and so what?"

"I've told you, I don't want to see you mixed up with women." He sighed deeply and, removing his cigar, spat on the rug. "Drop the chickens if you don't want me to drop you."

Rafael didn't argue back. He lowered his head. He finished dressing and then asked them to leave him alone for a moment while he prayed. They went out. A minute later the novillero joined his manager outside.

16

FUTILELY, LUIS TRIED TO GO TO SLEEP. THE
bed was hot and in his brain the same film was showing, time
after time. Even though he'd done nothing he felt exhausted.
He lit a new cigarette and with the match he looked at his
watch. Two thirty-five in the morning. The smoke had no
taste anymore and it burned his tongue.

The corrida had been terrible. Rafael had flopped shame-
fully, and one of the other matadors, Joselillo, was gored. That
was it. Rafaelillo was bad all afternoon and even though his
bulls were clearly the best he couldn't handle them. The audience came down on top of him, booing him unmercifully.
After he couldn't kill his last bull and the trained steers had
to come in to lead it out, Don Paco consoled him from behind
the fence.

"Don't worry, Rafael, you've still got three performances
coming up soon."

This is what really made Luis mad. Rafaelillo could in no
way justify a flop like that; perfect animals, no wind to blow
the capes, nothing. Who could be blamed then? That would
be the newspaper critics' problem. The following day the
city would read the bribed critics' versions of the events. God,
it made you burn with rage to see brave bulls, beautiful bulls,
ruined like that. Rafael doesn't belong near the fiesta brava
and yet here he is with three more fights coming up. And me?
Who am I to say this? But if I only had the chance — maybe
on one of those animals I could have cut ears and been carried out on the shoulders of the crowd.

This was the image of ultimate and glorious success — to be carried by the crowd from the plaza — and this wonderful, impossible warming picture of himself rarely left the back of his mind. With it would come everything, food, a steady place to sleep, security, love, and a splendid ornate monument over his mother's grave.

When he returned to the Hotel Montejo he had decided, once and for all, to become a torero no matter how: I don't want to be a half-man and live off women. But how was he to get free of Estela? He thought long on this, alone in this room, stretched out and smoking on the wretched bed. Estela was a rock in his pathway, Camioneto had said, a giant boulder that he'd have to detour around somehow. You're going to end up like him, Luis accused himself. You're going to end up like Rafaelillo. You'll just sink lower and lower and you'll wind up losing whatever pride you've got left. As Camioneto said, bullfighting is a religion and toreros have to respect the suit of lights. Did Rafaelillo, and the others who called themselves toreros just because they walked into a ring in a costume, respect it?

When his cigarette stub burned his fingers Luis cursed out loud. He decided, right then, to go for Estela and speak to her frankly. He dressed rapidly.

It was cold in the street, the piercing thin, chill of pre-dawn.

He kept arguing with himself. She — what the hell does he mean to you anyway? Fed up. Time to get rid of her. When you'd least expect it, when she got tired of you, she'd kick you out in the street. And then you'd be worse off than now . . .

He came to The Cricket. The other girls knew him now and asked if he was looking for Estela.

"Yes."

"Wait a while, she's with a customer."

"Tell her to come now."

He stayed there in the doorway with a new cigarette. The time crawled by. Finally, Estela came up behind him.

"What you want?"

"Let's go." Luis tossed away his cigarette and took her by the arm.

"What's bitten you?" She pulled back.

"Let's go," he repeated.

"I can't right now. I got one with real money. I can't leave him."

"Let's go!" Luis had forgotten any other words.

She crossed her arms. The green light that flooded down from the cabaret's sign, made her seem unreal, as though she were dead. Her body under the satin dress must have been stiff with the cold. The same lighting effect made her face a paintless mask with three sullen holes burned in it.

"Get going," she said. "I'll see you at the hotel."

Luis looked at her long and hard. Didn't she understand plain language? He was ordering her to come with him right now. Why was she refusing then?

Once more he told her: "Let's go — I want to talk to you!"

Unexpectedly, she drew herself up. With her hands on her hips, she shoved her stubborn jaw out at him.

"Get out of here and let me work!"

Hot fury of frustration began to boil inside Luis Ortega. Where did Estela get off talking like this? God, had he become so weak and so ineffectual he couldn't even make this buñí obey him?

The torero's fingers sunk into the girl's bare arm. He jerked her to him roughly.

"Let's go!"

"What's eating you?" Estela said between clenched teeth

as she struggled. "I told you I got a customer with money and I'm not going to let one of the others get him. What kind of a pimp are you anyway? If you're looking for money, for Christ's sake let me earn it!"

Luis knew that was the end. He let her go and looked hard at her. What could he do now? He thought of Camioneto. He knew that since their fight he had joined Juanito Lavín and that he slept nights in the place Juanito's mother ran over by the San Juan Market. He understood now, finally, that his friend of the hungry days had spoken the truth when he'd warned him of the danger that Estela was to him.

"A boulder in the path."

He must have said it out loud.

"What the devil are you talking about now?"

Luis shook his head.

"Nothing. I'm not talking about anything."

He spun on his heels and with his hands in his pockets, he walked off shaking his head as though to shake some bad idea out of it.

Estela watched him go, thin, hard, his chin down on his chest. Then she shrugged her shoulders and went back in The Cricket.

17

HE RECOGNIZED THEM IMMEDIATELY AND went to sit on the stirrup board a few feet away.

"Hola," he greeted them lightly.

"Hola," Juanito Lavín said in return.

But Camioneto didn't even turn around. They were working out. Luis felt tired, hungry, dead from lack of sleep. Since he'd left Estela in the doorway of the cabaret, he hadn't stopped walking. Subconsciously, his steps led to La Plaza México. It was barely eight and the cement stands still had the chill of night on them.

Camioneto was coaching Lavín, acting as the bull, pointing out his mistakes, advising him with the same interest he used to show in Luis. When he was crossing the arena Luis had been sure that his friend would come up to him, shake his hand, and say that everything was forgotten. That way it would be easy for both of them. And why don't you be the one to speak first? The question became more insistent as time passed. Camioneto hadn't turned to look at him once. Why's it have to be me? He recognized the voice of his pride. It was him after all who started it. Let him beg my pardon, then.

Juanito Lavín dropped the cape and grabbed the muleta. Camioneto was sweating heavily and while Juanito made passes at an imaginary bull, he took a rest. Luis stood up. The capes they were using were his.

"Juanito," he asked timidly. "Lend me the cape?"

"Grab it."

He unfolded it — his beloved cape — and went through the motions of a couple of verónicas. His head ached and his eyes felt as though they were swimming in tabasco. The cape weighed terribly and his arms were tiring.

"What a brute you are!" rasped a voice behind him.

It was a rough voice, a good voice, a voice as dear to him as a brother's. He turned quickly. Camioneto limped over to him, shaking his head disapprovingly. He snatched the cape out of his hands, withdrew a couple of yards, planted his feet apart on the sand, spread open the cape, and swung his arms.

"Don't you even know that the off hand is the one that finishes off the third part of the pass?" He spoke like a schoolteacher. "Have you forgotten how to hold your elbows? Forgotten that a verónica goes like this . . ."

In the morning's clear sun, the cape swung by Camioneto seemed to blossom like a magenta flower and it left in the warm air the colorful vision of a perfect verónica.

He ended with a half-verónica and after stalking away as gracefully as his lame leg would let him, he tossed the folded cape into Luis's hands and snarled: "All right, you now, let's go, and right where you're standing!" He bent over imitating a bull, and charged hard at the cloth which Luis held out.

18

IN THE DOORWAY OF THE BATHS OF JORDAN, Juanito Lavín said goodbye to them.

"We'll expect you for eats," said Camioneto.

"Thanks, mano."

An hour later they came out, clean and very talkative. The sun was beating down hard. The steam bath and the cold shower afterwards had completely revived Luis. He felt clean and new. Camioneto had given Luis a talking to in there — a rough one. And Luis took it without protest.

"It's all finished, Camioneto," he'd told him. "Finished. Now I'm going to do anything but just make me a torero."

Camioneto had grunted dubiously.

"It's all finished, honest. Don't even talk to me about women. I've enough for ten years."

They found themselves talking about Rafaelillo. Yes, Camioneto had also witnessed his shameful flop.

"Ought to be a warning to you," said Camioneto. "Just
the way he looked to you in La México yesterday, that bad
or worse, is the way you looked to me in Jojutla that day."

"I tell you it's going to be different."

They crossed San Juan de Letrán. The merry-go-round
horses of a little carnival were sleeping under their canvas
hoods.

"Let's go see the impresario," Luis suggested.

"What for? They going to give you a date?"

"If I'm lucky. Rafael introduced me to the doctor last
week and he told me to come see him."

Outside the office, a man in overalls with a pail of paste
and large brush was pasting a poster on the gray wall. They
stopped to read it.

"See the luck some people got?" said Luis bitterly. The
man finished pasting, stuck his brush in his belt like a general's
sword, and walked off.

The poster said:

REAPPEARANCE
OF
RAFAELILLO

Ahead of them were twenty youths all waiting to see the
impresario. They waved to Rodríguez across the way. Luis
sat down on the bundle and Camioneto leaned up against the
wall. An hour went by. Two hours.

During this time other young toreros had arrived and a few
managers. Inside the office would be jammed. Camioneto
nudged Luis.

"Come on. It's going to be tough to get to see him here."

He pointed to behind the little church on the corner. "The doctor parks his car over there. When he drives up, bam, we grab him."

They changed their waiting place. Luis felt hungry and he suggested they eat as soon as they'd seen the impresario. He had some money and he invited him to the Tupinamba.

"Save that parné for when you really need it," Camioneto advised him. "You haven't got anybody now to hand you more."

Luis flushed. Camioneto regretted this thrust and quickly said: "I'm getting my eats over at Lavín's place. His mother's bull happy, so she goes along with it fine. They're poor as hell but they won't miss an extra taco for you. Asks about you all the time. She likes you. Juanito told her how your old lady had him at her house before she died."

It was three o'clock when the impresario pulled up in his flaming Buick.

Luis was there in front of him in one bound.

"Doctor," he said timidly, doffing his cap, "I'm Luis Ortega."

"And so?" The impresario's voice was smooth but hard.

"You told me the other day to come see you. Remember? Rafaelillo spoke to you . . ."

"Ah yes." The impresario tried to smile. His thin mustache barely twitched.

"And here I am. I want to get put on one of these Sundays. I swear I'll give it everything I've got — I'll kill myself to cut ears . . ."

They were crossing the street. The impresario was striding along with big steps, Luis trotting beside him like a puppy. There was desperation in the boy's face; he had to land him in the few yards that were left before reaching the office. The Almighty was evasive.

"This year it won't be possible. Got all the openings signed up. Come to see me next year. And meanwhile — " he advised him — "get out in the small towns and fight all you can so that . . ."

Luis pulled up, realizing that there was nothing more to be said. "Next year." Uy, what a long ways off!

"But *then* you'll really put me on?"

"Right!"

At the entrance to the impresario's office they could see the familiar figure of Don Paco. Luis saw at a distance how this man was greeted, how he fell in behind the doctor and went in after him.

When he came back to Camioneto he was fuming.

"What happened, Luis?"

He spat out his anger. " 'Impossible this season, come see me next year — ' "

The two of them stood there silently. Camioneto grabbed up the bundle, stuck it under his arm, and said it was time to eat.

19

LIKE THE TIME BEFORE, RAFAELILLO HAD asked Luis to go to the Hotel Montejo to help him dress in exchange for a few pesos that he needed now as never before. Camioneto decided that since it was Sunday he'd sleep a little later.

It was three minutes to eleven when Luis knocked at Rafael's room. He heard voices inside, the sound of footsteps

and the snap as the lock was thrown back. From inside there
appeared the face of a red-haired woman.

"What'd you want?"

Confused, Luis looked first at the number of the room and
then at the woman.

"Excuse me," he asked, "Rafaelillo lives here?"

"Yes, what do you want him for?"

Someone must have asked from the bedroom what was going on because the woman turned her head to say that a boy
was asking for Rafael. Ortega heard him say to come in.

Luis went in. The blinds were drawn and a smoky haze
hung in the living room. He looked around: There were
bottles and half-filled glasses all over and cigarette butts and
ashes on the rug. With his cap in his hand, Luis stood there.
The girl glanced at his face and she smiled. She was a magnificent creature, flashily dressed.

"You're a torero also?"

"Yes, miss."

"Why does the matador want you, or what do you want
him for?"

"I don't want anything. I just came to arrange his things
for him."

In a moment Rafaelillo appeared at the bedroom door with
his red dressing gown and a cigarette in his hand. He waved
to Luis.

"How goes it?"

Luis replied fine.

"There're the things, champ." Rafaelillo pointed to them.
"The cape basket and all the rest."

"Rafael," Luis said, after looking after the capes, the muletas and the swords, "give me some parné for the votive
candles."

From his wallet Rafaelillo took out a bill and held it out to

Luis. Then he dressed quickly in a suit. The three of them left. Below, the watchman was polishing the Cadillac with a chamois.

"I'm going to the Villa, to pray to the Virgin," said Rafaelillo as he started the motor.

Luis pulled down his cap. "Right, Matador." God, to be honoring this man with that glorious title. "When you get back everything will be all ready."

He moved away. The girl, who hadn't got in, stuck her head through the window. Rafael put his face up for her to kiss.

"Not coming, Nancy?"

She shook her head.

"You go alone. I better get back to the house. The Bandit — she's going to be furious cause I didn't show up there for work last night."

Rafael shifted into low and smiled: "Anyway, you took care of your homework fine, darling."

As he started off Nancy waved. Her costume jewelry tinkled.

"Luck, my love — see you in the plaza."

20

HISTORY WAS REPEATED. RAFAEL, HIS TALENT as a torero only in evidence in his splendid uniform, flopped soundly. And once more Luis Ortega cried silently as he saw him waste two magnificent animals. What I would have liked to have tried to do with them, he kept thinking as he gathered together the novillero's things while the crowd whistled and booed. I swear I could do better if I had the chance!

After the fight, there was a party in Rafael's apartment. The place was jammed. While the torero was getting undressed, Luis felt very out of place. This is bullfighting? It just couldn't be. According to Camioneto the fiesta brava was sacrifice and the toreros were high priests of austere rites. And was this the fiesta brava then, this room full of misfits, these degenerates who revealed their true selves with no sense of shame or modesty — who praised a disastrous performance in exchange for a free drink?

If this was bullfighting, it was better to die of hunger.

What made him maddest were these friends of Rafaelillo's, who rationalized the flop, convincing him without too much trouble that he was the greatest torero in the world and that his reputation not only wasn't hurt but rather helped by that afternoon's disaster.

"Wasn't your fault, Rafael," piped one effete youth. "The bulls just gave out on you, just gave out that's all. Let you down, that's what they did. And the crowd was against you and you know why? 'Cause you've got personality, that's why, because they just can't *bear* your being right up there where you are. . . ."

Luis finished up his job. With his cap in his pocket, he slipped out of the place full of loathing and rage and impotence, without waiting for the handout Rafaelillo had promised him.

21

LETTERED ON THE DOOR THEY COULD READ:

Filogonio Martínez
Merchant
Zacapú, Mich.

Camioneto nodded. This was the truck they wanted. At noon La Merced market place reeked of vegetables, of grain, of feet, and of the sweat of unwashed bodies. They had been wandering around for hours in the huge market that supplied groceries to the city in search of a truck that would be heading for Michoacán. It was the month of country fairs in that state and it was too good a chance to lose.

The three of them had been working on the project since early morning. They had decided to go out and seek their fortune elsewhere, convinced now that in Mexico City they hadn't a prayer. Juanito Lavín told his mother that they were going to try their luck in the small towns and she agreed that it was a good idea. Not a tear from her eyes nor a word from her lips that wasn't encouragement.

"The only thing I want," the old taco vender had said as they left, "if you're going to be toreros is for you to be good ones. And don't be afraid of anything, except hunger. And above all, never a backward step!"

Luis felt a great warmth for her and he wished all bull-fighters' mothers could be like this; not like the rest of them who smothered their sons and got all tragic when they risked their necks a bit in front of the bulls. He transferred a good part of the love he had felt for his dead mother to this woman. If I get famous before Juanito, he thought, I'll get her out of this filthy hovel. I'll buy a house for her — a good big one in San Angel — and we'll all live there together, and Juanito and Camioneto and I will be like brothers and she'll have a servant to help her and doctors when she gets old and sick and she can die in the best hospital in Mexico City, and I'll have her buried near my mother with a monument almost as splendid.

In the doorway she had taken from her bosom a thin cluster of bills and handed them to Camioneto, who was the eldest of the three.

"Here you go. Thirty pesos. Might come in handy."

They decided, at Pancho's suggestion, to go to La Merced, where the trucks that brought the food to feed three million inhabitants always came. By experience he knew that the drivers were usually pretty good types as far as young toreros went and that if they could just find one they'd probably be able to talk him into it.

And they found one. In a loud shirt he was standing by the tailgate counting the sacks of grain that the loaders were heaving off the truck. He made a little check that looked like a bird on the loading form for each sack.

Camioneto went up to him, as the man wet the point of his pencil with saliva.

"You're from Zacapú, right? Well, that's where we're heading."

"That's tough. Not allowed to take passengers."

"We're not passengers, we're toreros."

"And so?"

Luis kept at him. "And so we could go — if you'll say the word."

Camioneto backed him up, pleading: "Give us a break. We'll even help you unload the truck."

This seemed a little more interesting to the driver.

"All right, get helping, and then we'll talk."

They never would have believed then that truck had so many and such heavy sacks. An hour later when the last sack was down, Camioneto went up to the driver, sweating and barely able to breathe.

"There you go, boss — at your service!" He wiped the sweat off his dripping face.

"All right," said the man calmly. "And now the money."

"Money? I thought you said — "

"I said unload and then we'd talk, and that's what we're doing. You worked off half the trip — now cough up the rest if you want to go."

Camioneto and the driver launched into an argument. Finally Luis and Juanito saw their friend take out the little roll of bills and peel off ten pesos for the driver.

Pancho came back to them and told them to get in the truck. They filled up with gasoline and bounced off heading out of the City of Mexico.

22

WHEN THEY ARRIVED, ZACAPU LOOKED ITS best. There was excitement in the town, excitement in the music, the crowds in their Sunday best, the food and alcohol, the laughter and the fireworks. They shook the driver's hand, and with their capes folded under their arms they set off to see the plaza. Luis felt wonderful. He was back with Camioneto and now his "brother" Juanito was there to complete the three musketeers. And there was bullfighting in the offing! Who could ask for anything more? The pain of Estela hurt very little now; women really weren't very important.

They found the plaza off to the side of the main square. It was a makeshift thing and lacked burladero shields. They peeped into the corral. There were four animals with enormous horns; among them, the biggest, was a terrible brown animal with black vertical stripes.

They asked who was the impresario, and nobody could tell them. Some said it must be the mayor, others the priest, and others thought it was the chief of the militia.

The boys went to the square and sat on a bench. The corrida was only sixty minutes away now.

"Look who's coming," Juanito said suddenly.

They saw a tall thin youth dressed in the classic costume of aspirant toreros — tight trousers cut in the Valencia style, the shirt knotted at the waist, a scarf around the neck, a cap of small black and white checks. He walked along fast followed by two others.

"What's up, Tato?" Juanito greeted him.

The one called Tato stopped, surprised, and then his surprise turned to pleasure.

"Hey, Juanito! When did you get here?"

Lavín pointed to his friends. "We just got here. From Mexico City. Going to see if we can't sneak in a pass or two with the bugs. And you?"

Tato took out a crumpled package of cigarettes and offered some to the boys.

"I'm in a mess, a real mess. I'll probably be in jail an hour from now."

"How come? What did you do?"

"It was the fault of a ball-less bastard. See, they talked to me in Mexico City about coming here to fight in the fair. I asked two hundred pesos and they gave it to me. Well, this guy comes crying and begging for me to take him along as the other fighter on the program. Sure, I tell him, but you have to chip in on the expenses, so he comes through with fifty maracas. We got here yesterday. This morning he gets one look at the animals and takes off. Just found out he went out on the bus."

"And so what's the problem?" asked Camioneto.

There was desperation in Tato's face. "Only that if there aren't two matadors, me and another, they're going to throw us in jail. Neither of these bums," he pointed to the two boys with him, "want to have anything to do with those animals."

Luis was going to say something but Juanito stopped him with his elbow. Blowing the ashes off his cigarette, he said casually, "I might be able to help you. I could fight."

"You?"

"Yes, and these fellows would help me."

"Well, it's done then!" Tato breathed deeply with relief. "Then we'll see each other before the fight starts."

He was starting to go off when Juanito took him by the arm.

"Hey, not so fast. We still got to settle something."

"What?"

"They paid you two hundred to fight in the fair. The other guy slipped you another fifty. So you're paying us how much? Because don't get the idea we're going to fight free."

"Don't big-deal me — "

"We're talking business."

And they talked business heatedly for fifteen minutes. Tato wouldn't go over ten pesos. Juanito demanded fifty. They were deadlocked until Juanito shrugged his shoulders.

"We'll bring you some cigarettes when you're in jail," he said as a farewell, and he and Luis and Camioneto started off.

Tato caught up with them.

"Don't act like that, Juanito. We're toreros and we can work this out. You're asking too much."

"There's nothing more to say. Either it's fifty pesos or nothing doing."

There was no time for further argument. Tato took some bills out of his pocket. He counted out five of them and handed them to Juanito. He took him by the arm.

"Come on, let's get dressed. Got a uniform?"

"No."

"Well — I'll lend you one."

Before they could get dressed, the toreros had to lure the bulls from the corrals into the stalls so they'd be ready to charge into the ring when the toril was opened. While they were getting everything ready in back, wetting down the capes and muletas, the people began to fill up the stands of the little arena. They could hear the sour sounds made by the band as it attacked some helpless march. Somewhere meat snacks were being fried and the greasy smoke drifted back to them.

"As soon as this is over," Juanito said as Luis helped him wrap the sash around his waist, "I swear to God that I'm going to eat for three days in a row."

Juanito's face was wet with sweat.

"Juanito," said Tato, and Juanito turned. "Juanito, you'll go first, won't you?"

"All right," he answered. Then he looked at Luis and shrugged his shoulders. "Why not?"

The bleat of the cornet announcing that the performance was about to start hit them like a knife thrust. Their faces suddenly drained of all color and the saliva dried in their mouths. "Never a backward step" was the last thing Juanito managed to say as he headed for the cuadrilla gate next to El Tato.

They paraded out across the ring. The crowd howled drunkenly. Luis, Camioneto, and the other two friends of Tato's distributed themselves around the ring.

On the crossbars over the gate where the bull would come in the keeper of the toril waited for the signal from the mayor to let in the first animal. From the place occupied by the authorities of the town came the signal in the form of the waving of a red handkerchief. There was a great shout when the big striped bull shot out of the gate. From the first testing pass, given from a long way away and with jittering feet, Luis saw that the ugly animal wasn't "clean," that it had been caped before. It hooked badly on both sides. He was suddenly very fearful for this friend he liked so much.

"Be careful with this one," Luis pleaded. "This one's bad, Juanito."

"Get going!" Tato said, giving Juanito a push.

Juanito stepped out into the ring. The striped animal, upon seeing the cape, hurled itself toward him like a locomotive. Juanito felt the ground shaking under his feet, but he didn't take a step back. Tricked by the cape, the animal passed by the first time, but then from the second on it began veering in toward the man's body until the torero had to give ground and save himself by running behind the fence.

"Get out and fight him!" yelled the mob. "Don't run!"

"Hey, capitán," yelled one, "go out and screw your feet into the ground!"

Go out and screw your mother into the ground, Juanito thought, his eyes blazing at the last shouter. It was a dark Indian, drunk and noisy who in spite of the sweltering heat wore a heavy overcoat of coffee-colored wool.

There were no picadors to help him. Tato reminded him

there weren't going to be any when Juanito commented that three good jabs by a good picador would help this animal to behave.

The crowd was yelling for action, and Juanito, to give them a little, grabbed up a pair of banderillas. As he went by Luis said to him: "Get them in any way you can and then get out of there!"

Lavín went out to the bull with the sticks in one hand. He showed off his skill and athletic ability very well as he dodged around and serpentined in front of the animal in preparation for the actual placing. Then in the center of the ring he started his trip in, and as he and the bull came together perfectly, he barbed the sticks into the bull's shoulders and spun away. The loud applause rang wonderfully in his ears.

When he grabbed the second pair, Camioneto ordered: "Dedicate these to the presidente of the ring — if we're lucky he'll slip you some eating money."

Juanito went out under the box and dedicated the pair of banderillas. The mayor, fat and dressed in black, took off his hat in acknowledgement.

The pair was good. And the third pair also, although a little far apart. I can get a fight out of him, Juanito was saying to himself as he came over to the fence. He charges plenty hard but he isn't so vicious. Just a question of bluffing him out on the right side. He took a gulp of water, grabbed the muleta, and went out toward the bull.

"Face-fight him, face-fight him!" Luis warned him frantically. "No fancy stuff!"

But Juanito had his own plan. It was fixed firmly in his brain that the striped beast would pass correctly if he could just train him how to do it. He walked out in front of the bull, and before he knew it he had knelt down on both knees. The crowd, on its feet now, let out a yell.

"No!" yelled Luis from the fence. "No, Juanito!"

They were awful, those moments, the most terrible that Juanito had gone through in his life, the worst he ever would go through. As soon as he felt his knees on the sand he had the immediate urge to get off them. There was still time — the bull still hadn't charged. But what if he stood up now? It seemed to him that he heard over the roar of the crowd his mother's voice: "Never take a backward step." Forward then — he'd have to go forward, cross over the line of the intended charge of this lousy half-breed, now that he'd decided to try to fight it on his knees.

The bull lunged. It was like sitting in the path of a locomotive roaring down the tracks at sixty miles an hour. With its horns sticking way out at the same level as the torero's face, the hair along its neck bristling, the hoofs digging deep into the soft ground, the nostrils distended and wheezing like a factory whistle, the black striped creature bore down closer and closer to the boy. Suddenly there passed in front of Juanito's eyes a flash of something brown or red or some color, and at the same time there was a great howl from the mob.

Oh, God, it went by, he managed to think. But the bull was already wheeling around. When it found itself tricked by the cape, it had braked with its front feet, whirled around and was charging again. It all happened so fast that Juanito had no time — no time to change his position, to change the angle of the bull's charge as he knew it should be changed. Astonished, frightened by his own courage, he had remained unmoving as though made of stone, the muleta cape still held high.

It had to happen and it did.

A great gasp came from the crowd. Then immediately a guffaw, tremendous, prolonged, incredible — the thrilling, guilty delight in the morbid. For Juanito Lavín was flying very high in the hot afternoon. He flew through the air like a sponge in the wind, weightlessly it seemed, like emptiness in the stomach. They all ran to the rescue. Luis and Camioneto dragged the torero away. Tato lured the bull off to one side.

They carried the wounded boy off behind the fence, out to the corral where they had dressed. It stank of manure and of sweetly sour hay.

Anxiously, Camioneto examined the wound. He paled when his hand went in up to the wrist. He raised his eyes. Luis begged the truth.

"Rough one?"

"Terrible. A bitch of a wound."

Camioneto shouted to the other young torero, who had come with them, to run and find a doctor. He came back in a moment saying there wasn't one, only the druggist on the other side of the street. Quickly they spread out a cape and on it they laid Juanito. Grabbing the cape by the corners they improvised a stretcher.

"Lift him up!"

Almost running, they carried him along, leaving a thin red trail of agony on the ground behind them. "It's a hole they're never going to be able to fill — he might kick off — hurry." Camioneto knew the truth; he'd seen bad horn wounds, but never one like this. "Must be just like the one that killed Alberto Balderas." Yes, like that one. The horn had torn and ripped the torero's intestines.

They banged on the door with their fists. A woman came out with a frightened face. "Got to see the doctor," Camioneto blurted out, "quick!"

The woman looked at the blood pooling in the cape. She shook her head.

"Later — he's sleeping."

"Call him!" Luis snarled like a bulldog. He shoved the woman to one side and went in, followed by the others. They laid Juanito on a mahogany table. A thread of blood began trickling down to the tiles of the floor. A few moments went by. They turned when they heard the footsteps of a thin old man.

He worked his toothless jaws.

"What you want?"

Camioneto stepped to the side so that the man could see Juanito.

"He's wounded."

"Knifed?"

"No. A bull gored him. Barely five minutes ago in — "

"I don't want to get mixed up in anything," the man shrilled. "Get him out of here."

"Fix him up!"

The little man pulled back, snapping his gums together.

"I can't. I'm not a doctor, just a druggist. Take him someplace else."

A man was dying with a horn-shattered belly and this old man refused to help him. Where the hell would they take him — all the way to the hospital? Camioneto knew he'd die on the way. His hand went to his waist and he pulled out the puntilla dagger used to give the bulls the coup de grace.

"I say you're going to fix him," he threatened, "or I'm going to open you up."

The druggist blinked. Then he shrugged his shoulders and shuffled over to the shelves of medicines. Camioneto escorted him, the knife blade close to the man's curved, bony back.

Luis Ortega stayed close to Juanito holding his hand. Tato's friend had returned to the plaza. Outside was a curious crowd that tried to get in the pharmacy. The druggist's wife locked the door. The wounded boy shuddered, moaning. His eyes flickered open.

It took him some long moments to finally focus on Luis. He tried to smile.

"Passed me fine — first time," he faltered. "Then, couldn't get him to — "

His face contracted with pain. His trembling hands clutched at the well of blood that was his stomach. He must have felt the wet warmth because he pulled his hands away and held them up to look at them. He kept looking at them for a long time. They were two red Christmas Eve flowers.

"Is — is it a rough one — this slash?"

"No. It's nothing. Doctor's coming now."

"Luis." Juanito Lavín dug his nails into Ortega's arm. "Luis, more than I can take — I can't take — this much, Luis. I'm hurting bad — everything's going black. I really think I'm going to kick off now."

"Don't talk crazy," said Luis, trying to keep Juanito from seeing the fright in his face and the tears in his eyes.

The druggist came back. To one side of Juanito's body he placed two glass containers: alcohol and iodine, all he had for emergencies. He told them to uncover the wounded man. While Luis opened his pants, Camioneto took out of the mouth of the wound the handkerchief with which he had tried to stop the hemorrhaging.

It was a blackening, shocking crater. Luis felt he was going to faint, and he turned his face away. Camioneto just clenched his jaws.

Juanito looked up at Camioneto's face which was leaning so strangely over his.

"Pancho — I've kicked off already — when you see my old lady tell her — tell her I died like she would have wanted — walking forward! Tell her what happened — tell her I took a hole in me rather than let her down. Didn't make it, Camioneto — I couldn't be a matador — but I died like a matador. Keep telling Luis — not to worry about this — this here. The bull doesn't wound, Pancho — the wounds, the bad ones, they're handed out by hunger — "

The druggist uncorked the bottle of alcohol and sloshed some down into the wound. Juanito shrieked once and his torn body twisted in a convulsion. Then he slipped into a blessed faint.

Luis sprang to his side.

"Is he dead, doctor?" he asked in anguish.

The druggist held his ear against the boy's chest.

"No, but it won't be long."

Taking advantage of the faint, he washed the wound with more alcohol and then turned up the bottle of iodine and emptied it into the wound. He left some chunks of cotton inside the gaping wound.

"Almost like a Caesarian," he said in a professional tone.

They didn't know what a Caesarian was but the man's tone told them it was something very serious.

"Will he make it, doctor?"

The man was cleaning off his fingers with a piece of cotton dipped in alcohol. "Afraid not. His guts are in shreds."

Juanito came to again. Nothing hurt now. He felt good now, serene, almost carefree. Why did the fellows have such scared faces? He tried to smile. Now he understood everything. The best moment in life is the one just before death.

"Boys," he whispered, "I've kicked off, and there's no helping it. In my pants pocket is the parné that Tato gave us. Me — what good's it going to do me? Take it and head for some new place."

"Thanks, Juanito. The three of us will be spending it together soon, you'll see."

Juanito smiled again. He took Luis's hand.

"And you, boy," he said, "don't ever get scared. You can make yourself into a matador, a great one. And like my old lady says, never a backward step . . ."

When that long silence came they knew Juanito Lavín was

dead. On his face was a look of satisfaction. Just as though he'd been awarded a lap around the ring, Luis thought.

"Well," said the druggist, "now he *is* dead!"

Just then there was a pounding at the door. The woman went to open it, drying her hands on her apron. Before unlocking she glanced over at her husband.

"Go on, open it," he ordered.

Three men in khaki uniform came in.

"All right," one of them barked, "where are these toreros?"

"Here," said Camioneto standing in front of them.

Two of the three grabbed him by the arms and started to drag him off.

"Get a move on then, the bullfight isn't over yet."

Luis sprang to help his friend. "We can't go back, señores. We can't. Look — " and he pointed to Juanito's body.

The officers let Camioneto go and crossed over to the table. "What happened to him?"

The druggist answered.

"God took him away. He just died."

The eyes of the men in uniform widened. They looked at the blood that was still seeping to the floor, and they took off their caps.

"Ah," they said, "all right."

And then they left.

23

FROM HER WINDOW THE WOMAN WITH THE graying hair, pale and stately in her widowhood, saw the three men in uniform come up and knock on the door of the pharmacy. She also saw how the door opened and they went inside. She saw an old woman in a black shawl among the group of curious people hovering around.

She called to her.

"What's happening there?" Her voice was hard, authoritative.

The other woman smiled up at her. "Haven't you heard? There's a dead one here."

"So the drinking and brawling has really begun!"

"Nothing like that, Doña Carolina." The woman in black had come over to the window and her skinny fingers wrapped themselves around the grillwork like roots. "Nothing of the sort. The dead one's a boy. One of the toreros."

"Poor man!"

"But he wasn't even a man," the old one corrected her. "He was just a boy. His friends don't even have any way to bury him."

24

"WHAT I'D LIKE TO KNOW," WHINED THE druggist, never stopping his toothless gums from chomping, "is who's going to pay for the treatment, that's what I'd like to know."

Nobody listened to him. Nobody listened because the young toreros were waiting for the words that now would never be spoken by the boy who lay there lifelessly, calm, and peaceful on the cape. It struck Luis that the cape with its yellow lining was like a great open flower, the flower of Juanito's death.

People were crowding in now with small noises and eyes of surprise, fouling the air, changing the smell in the small room to one of sweat and feet. The toreros, nevertheless, felt alone, terribly alone in the middle of that ring of people. Juanito made it, Luis was thinking, no matter how, he made it safe to the burladero.

"Feet first," Camioneto muttered. "How come we all go out feet first?"

Luis thought of Juanito's mother, of that woman who had wanted a bullfighter for a son. Just the day before she'd seen him so alive. What would she say now if her eyes could see this wretched room in this little town? Somebody's got to tell her what's happened. He could write her a letter tonight. In his terrible and painful handwriting, he could tell her that Juanito died like the great toreros, with not a backward step. That would console her. By god, he thought, I will become a great matador and I will buy that house for her and treat her as though she were my own mother and make it all up to her for what she'd suffered and was going to suffer!

Mechanically he took the muleta, unfolded it, and covered Juanito's body with it. Then he stood by the corpse, his head down on his chest.

A finger poked at his shoulder.

"Hey, young man, what I want to know is who's going to take care of all this?"

He turned his head and looked at the druggist. He felt like spitting in his face. Couldn't he see how they felt? Couldn't he just shut up? How the hell did he know how the stupid bill was going to be paid?

The old man belched. "I want you to take him out of here now. Don't want him here any longer."

Then the room buzzed unexpectedly. Heads turned around. The woman who had been watching from the window came in followed by two individuals.

"What's going on?" she asked.

The druggist wiped the unpleasant expression off his face. Bowing, he said: "Doña Carolina!"

"What's happening?"

When the druggist pointed a trembling finger at the body the woman's hard eyes softened momentarily. She had a brief flash of an unforgettable scene from long ago, of her son, just a boy, lying riddled by the rebels' bullets, lying on a red blanket and making it redder and redder.

"He died on us," stammered the druggist.

Beside the corpse, Luis and Camioneto were crying. The woman went over to them. Her hand caressed Luis's head.

"Did he come with you?"

Luis barely could get the words out, "Yes, señora . . ."

"Where are you going to have the wake?"

"We — we don't know, señora."

"Are you from around here?"

"From Mexico City," said Camioneto. "We came here this noon to fight."

The druggist came up, his suspenders dangling down around his flanks.

"I just would like to know who's going to take care of the treatment costs."

The toreros shook their heads dumbly.

"We don't have any money. That's why we were fighting — to make some."

"Don Eulalio," the woman's voice snapped, "don't be a bore. Leave them alone."

The druggist looked crestfallen but he didn't speak again.

"If you don't have a place for the wake," Doña Carolina said to the boys gently, "you can use my house."

"Thank you, señora, but we don't have any money."

"It is not a matter of money." She clapped her hands to call the two men with her. "Espiridión and Angel — bring the body."

The men grabbed two corners of the cape and Luis and Camioneto took the other two. They went out into the street. In the plaza de toros the fight was still going on. As they crossed the little square they could hear the sour notes of the band and the shouts of the audience. Some curious people fell in behind them.

25

AT FOUR IN THE MORNING THE MAYOR arrived. He was very drunk. Eyes glazed, he tendered his respect and sympathy.

"But what's to be done?" he asked of no one in particular. "That bull's wounded a lot of people. But I promise you we won't allow him to fight next year."

He drank a cup of coffee and said goodbye. As he shook hands with Luis, he left two bills in his hand.

"Take these fifteen pesos, little present."

In the high-ceilinged room there were five other people besides Luis and Camioneto. Three were women who sobbed as though the corpse belonged to them. There was the smell of candlewax and perspiration. The toreros were lost in thought, with hollow eyes and the bitter taste of grief in their mouths.

It was the first time Luis had seen a young death; it was ugly. When fighting one saw death, of course, riding there on the horns; but that was a live, intelligent, sharp, polished death. Something to be tricked, something you gambled with, and competed with, gracefully, sportingly, artistically. A man was dressed in gold and silk then, and he wasn't alone but surrounded by people whom he cheated because he fooled them and didn't get killed. And you prepared yourself for death by making thousands of pesos so you could get killed a millionaire. When a real matador died there were always poems written and songs composed. Yes, because his death was a rich, elegant one. But this ragged, dark, unsung, small-town death — was this a rich, elegant death?

Luis never thought death was like this. He always thought it was like lightning, a blinding light that came and went without a trace. He knew now that death smelled, that it is born the very moment life ended: Won't death die sometime? And if it does die, what would its cadaver look like?

Juanito's body lay there on the floor, long, with the toes pointing one east and the other west. Doña Carolina had told the carpenters to make the coffin early, at dawn. Juanito was still on the cape and under the muleta. Since bringing him to the house several people had come to see him; many prayed and left some coins beside him, as though the ticket to the other world had to be paid for. Luis asked himself: Why does everyone feel sorry for the dead and not for the living?

At five o'clock the two carpenters arrived. They left their tools and some planks of pine in the vestibule. They said the Lord's Prayer and then measured the body for length and width. Then they set to work.

The day was gray. Around eight o'clock it began to drizzle steadily. If it were a fight day, it'd be called off, Luis thought. But you can't call off a burial.

Doña Carolina had them served breakfast. Death had killed their appetites and they barely tasted the chocolate and biscuits.

When they got up, Camioneto took the ones left on the

plate and was stuffing them in his pocket when his eyes met Luis's reproachful glance.

"For later," Camioneto mumbled.

They put the body in the coffin and they carried it uncovered outside. They waited a long time until the priest came.

"Let's go," said Doña Carolina, quietly.

Just a few people went along with Juanito to the cemetery. Some dark and ragged children trotted beside Camioneto.

"You're a torero, aren't you?" they asked.

"Yes."

"And him over there — " they pointed to the coffin swaying on the shoulders of the servants — "is he a torero too?"

"Yes."

"And how come they're going to bury him?"

The dogs came along too, several of them, wet and droopy, appearing from noplace. In the doorways the curious people watched the procession, crossing themselves and shaking their heads as though it seemed incredible that a torero could die.

The grave was no wider than a crate that they used to transport the bulls from the ranch to the ring. The men carrying death on their shoulders lowered it to one side of the hole. The rain gave Juanito's yellow face beads of perspiration. The priest prayed. Everything was done now. Doña Carolina nodded at Espiridión to signal him to put the cover on the coffin.

Juanito, Camioneto thought, he's going with his bullfighting uniform on.

Then, in the gray morning, Espiridión's hammering began. One, two, three. Always three clean, exact, blows to bury the nail into the wet wood.

"Hey." Camioneto elbowed Luis in the ribs.

"What?"

"You get the parné?"

"What parné?"

One, two, three. Three blows. Another nail in the coffin.

"What do you mean what parné? What the guy gave us."

Luis had forgotten until then that Juanito had told them to take the money from his pants pocket.

"No, I thought you . . ."

"Stupid!"

"Now it's too late."

"We got to get it."

"Leave it. They're going to bury him now."

"Like hell I will. Parné is parné and I'm not going to toss it away."

"Look," said Luis, counting the hammer blows of each nail, "it's all done."

Camioneto scratched his head.

"We got to get it out. It's no use to him. We're alive — we can use it for the wars."

Camioneto leapt over beside the grave and grabbed the hammer from Espiridión's hands.

"What is happening?" said the priest in alarm as he saw Camioneto start to yank out the nails which had just been so firmly driven in. "What is happening here?"

"Nothing, Father," Camioneto said. "Just forgot something — "

Three minutes later the top was off. Everyone stared as Camioneto reached into Juanito's pockets. They heard him grunt as he tried to roll the corpse over on its side. Another interminable minute went by.

Finally Camioneto straightened up smiling with something in his hand. He wiped the sweat off his forehead with his sleeve.

"All right now, Don Espiridión," he said handing back the hammer, "nail her up."

The servant again began to nail on the cover. Camioneto came back over to Luis and showed him the money.

"See how easy?" he whispered. "He was always a good guy, Juanito — he wouldn't mind our borrowing it off him."

Suspending it by two lassos, Espiridión and Angel lowered the coffin down to the bottom. The priest prayed once more and all knelt. Doña Carolina took a little handful of dirt and tossed it down on the box. Camioneto imitated her.

When Luis threw his down, he felt that with the bit of dirt went part of his own being.

26

IN BRIGHT COLORS THE POSTER PROCLAIMED:

LORENZO GARZA Y GREGORIO GARCÍA
Mano a mano!
4 Toros de la Punta 4

This poster was the first thing they saw when they got down off the truck that had given them a lift from Guadalajara. Dumfounded, they stood there looking at it and a wave of anger came over Luis. He whirled on Camioneto.

"Look what we've come all this way for!"

Camioneto was abject. "How the devil did I know it was a regular fight?"

"You could have asked!"

"I just heard there were fights — I never thought a little own like Jalostotitlán could have a big star like Garza."

"They'd never let me get near one of their bulls, much less ry a cape pass. And to think we could have maybe hitched a ride someplace else where there'd be something for us."

"Where?" Camioneto challenged.

"I don't know. Anyplace else but here."

The truth was that in the month or so since Juanito had been killed they'd managed to find only one chance to fight and that was in the tiny village of Teocaltiche — and Camioneto had been the one to fight. Well, not fight exactly. It was a comic stunt on the program. They'd offered Camioneto five pesos to lie on his back, his feet in the air, and with a bucket of soot balanced on them. Then they turned loose a bull. Normally, as in the famous Don Tancredo stunt, if the man stayed absolutely still a real toro bravo would not charge an inanimate object. However, this was not a fighting bull; it was a tame bull with turpentine thrown onto its testicles just before it came into the ring to make it charge. In its blind painful fury it would have crashed into a marble statue. It tossed Camioneto sky high and knocked him unconscious. But people threw down money to them and that plus five pesos made the bruises feel better.

So actually, though it was very disappointing to find out they wouldn't get a chance to fight here in this town, there was no other place they knew of right now where a pachanga was going on.

They wandered around town until twelve. Then they went to the corrals behind the plaza de toros to watch the drawing. They saw the representatives of the two matadors come as well as the authorities and many aficionados. They saw them pair off the bulls, putting the largest two with the smallest two, and then saw them draw lots. The bulls were big and handsome, but most of the horns were defective and dangerous compared to what one would see in Mexico City. Luis especially liked one. It was the albaio, the yellowish white one, the largest of all, and Garza's man drew it.

"God," said Luis as he watched the beautiful animals admiringly. "Wouldn't you give anything to see the fight — a real fight?"

"I'll take care of it for you."

"You crazy? We haven't that kind of money?"

"Who said anything about paying? Follow me."

They drifted away from the people and Camioneto found a spot to squeeze into the plaza under the stands. They found a small place under the stands where they could crouch and be hidden. They stayed cramped there for four hours, Luis dreaming about the albaio and wishing Juanito were there with them; the truth was that in the last month Juanito and his mother were never very far from Luis's thoughts.

At five minutes of four, they slipped out unnoticed and sneaked up through the jammed stands to some empty seats.

27

AS GREGORIO GARCIA RAN AROUND THE arena, smiling up at the applauding audience and triumphantly holding up the ear of the second bull of the afternoon, Luis turned to Camioneto and said with no change of expression: "I'm jumping in on the next one."

Camioneto's eyes widened. "You're what?"

"Give me the muleta!"

"Are you crazy? Number three is the biggest of all!"

"And that's why. I'm sick of being pushed around by half-breed oxen and scrawny steers! Now I want to see what it feels like to fool around with a real fighting bull."

Camioneto had suddenly become nervous. "Listen," he whispered, "the police are the ones who are going to do the fooling around if you try it. You know what they do to *espontáneos.*"

"It'll be worth it."

The presidente of the corrida gave the signal for the third bull of the afternoon to be let into the ring. Luis's heart began to bang against the inside of his ribs and only he understood what Lorenzo Garza was feeling in those moments as the matador rested his chin on the fence and watched the big toril gate clang open.

With his mouth dry Luis rasped: "Give me that muleta!"

And Camioneto saw such determination in Luis Ortega's eyes that he passed the muleta cape to him under his knees without protest.

The bull blasted out of the tunnel, its yellowish white hide gleaming in the late sun. Then things happened quickly. The bull hadn't even reached the center of the ring when Luis threw his muleta down into the ring and then followed it himself with a tremendous leap. The crowd gave a great gasp of surprise and anticipation as they saw him run out to meet the bull, the muleta spread in his right hand. He got down on his knees as the bull charged, and as the huge beast roared past him, he stayed there unmoving and defiant. A yell burst from the crowd. The bull wheeled and passed again. And then again, the boy still on his knees. And then again. And still again! The crowd was screaming with delight. He stood up, removed the stick from the muleta, and cited for the dangerous natural pass. The bull charged and Luis executed a slow, classic natural. As the bull came to the end of the pass it turned — the wrong way. Now it headed back towards him at a bad angle, and Luis saw it coming swerving dangerously. "Never a backward step," he heard Juanito's voice say. In that split second he had two choices: stand still or break and run for the fence. He chose the former.

He felt a sickening blow, like a tremendous punch, in his left leg, and then, as though some savage force were casting him into infinity, he experienced an awful sensation of being jerked up by the roots like a tree and hurled into the air. Everything spun, the world, his thoughts, everything.

When he crashed down to the ground the pain stabbed again. Dazedly he heard shouts, screams, curses, laughs, bellows — but he felt no fear; not because he was brave or because there was no pain, but simply because there was no time.

When they carried him to the passageway and stood him up, he shook his head. He was groggy from the pounding and he knew his nose was gushing blood. Then, suddenly, he was struck on the jaw. It wasn't a bull's horn, but a man's fist — the fist of a policeman armed with a Mauser rifle. Futilely he tried to ward off the blows that rained on him as several pairs of rough hands subdued him.

"Leave him alone," howled the crowd, "let him go!"

But they dragged him struggling down the passageway, slapping and punching him as they went. Out in the street they worked him over with their quirts as they hauled him like a wild animal to the jail.

In the arena Lorenzo Garza was starting his faena with the great yellowish bull. It had to be a good performance if he was to get any applause today, because the crowd was spoiled by the remarkable things the espontáneo had done. Yes, it had to be a great faena. Garza felt the pressure and gave it to them. The olés resounded in the clear blue afternoon sky, and in the breast of Luis Ortega they echoed, as in a cavern.

But you never took a backward step! he told himself. He tried to wipe away some of the blood from his face and he hung from the bars of the high window of the wretched cell where they'd thrown him.

28

THE SWORD BOY STUCK HIS HEAD OUT OF THE
hotel room a moment after Camioneto had knocked.

"What do you want?"

"See the matador."

"What about? He's getting dressed."

"It's a personal matter."

"Not now. Maybe when he goes down to eat."

Camioneto could hear the laughter and the talk going on
inside. Lorenzo had cut ears and tail off the bull that the
espontáneo, Luis Ortega, had really discovered with his
bravery. The faena that Garza put up with the animal was
glorious, solemn and honest, and if it had happened in Mexico
City the people would have raved about it for a year. The
boy had really caused it, because Garza would have much
preferred to take it easy in this little town and not strain
himself or take any useless risks. Instead he had to go out
there and eat the bull alive as though he were a young novillero again. Camioneto didn't know how Garza might re-
ceive him — or whether he'd even speak to him. Throwing
oneself into the ring during a big star's performance was a
serious offense, unforgivable. But Camioneto had gone to
the jail and they hadn't even let him see Luis. The police
chief hadn't even listened to his pleas.

"One hundred pesos to turn him loose," he had said.

One hundred pesos! This was an incredible amount of
money to even say, much less possess. Camioneto promised

that they'd both get right out of town and stay out, but the man was deaf to his pleas.

"One hundred pesos or fifteen days locked up."

Then when Camioneto left the jail the idea came to him to try to see Garza. Maybe he wasn't such a big star that he couldn't remember way back when he was struggling to make a name for himself.

Now Camioneto could see that the table was ready and awaiting the matadors in the hotel's small dining room. It was a large table and Camioneto counted places for ten people.

It was almost eight o'clock and Camioneto was crouched down on the stairs waiting, his dirty cap in his hand. God, he was thinking, the passes Luis pulled off with that bull.

They were good, they were marvelous. He could see the figure of Luis again, transfigured out there, brilliant, brave, serene, and unmoving in front of that great hunk of lethal muscle. And lord, how that old Big Nose Garza had to sweat and work to get the public to cheer him and to stop clamoring for the espontáneo to come back!

"This is the fellow, Matador," said a voice behind him. It was the voice of the sword boy.

Camioneto jumped up. He saw before him an ugly face, ugly but pleasant, and with bright smiling eyes, the face of the great Garza. The unlighted cigar that jutted from his teeth didn't even wobble as he said: "Who are you?"

Swallowing, Camioneto started: "It's about him — the espontáneo, Matador. . ."

"What's the matter with him?"

"He is in the web, Matador. I'm his manager — and I want to get him out."

"Ah!" said Garza with a little smile, and removing the cigar. "So you're the one who sent him out there to make me look bad."

"I told him not to do it, but he didn't pay any attention."
Garza looked at him with those penetrating eyes.

"He's got guts, that kid of yours."

"And he'll be a great torero. That's why I'm asking for your help, Matador."

"Well," said Garza, "wait until I eat and then we'll go get him."

29

IT WAS VERY EASY FOR GARZA TO OBTAIN Luis's release. He simply said: "I've come for the boy."

Five minutes later they were all three walking back to the hotel.

"You could become a great torero, boy," Garza said. "You've got the important part — the guts. Of course, you still have plenty to learn."

"The hard part is getting a chance, Matador."

"It is hard, I know. But the chances will come. I knocked around and went hungry a long time myself. Where do you head for now?"

"We don't know. Maybe there are some fights in the towns around here."

At the entrance to the hotel he stopped. He looked at them thoughtfully a moment. Then he took out his wallet, and extracted a twenty-peso bill.

"Here you go, lad," he said holding it out to Luis. "For the road."

He turned and walked away. Luis stayed there with his

mouth open. Twenty whole pesos! So there were some decent people in the bull world after all. It was too good to be true.

They ordered a splendid luncheon of beer and enchiladas at a booth on the street and Luis thought long on Garza and of the happenings of the past twenty-four hours.

"God, I was scared when I jumped in the arena."

"Don't tell me, I could see it in your face."

"But once down there on my knees, I wasn't scared."

Camioneto washed down the last of the enchilada with his beer. "Let's go."

"Let me pay first," Luis protested.

"Don't be stupid," said Camioneto under his breath. The girl had her back to them as she waited on another customer. "Let's go — fast. I hear a freight train!"

30

SOMETHING SHARP AND HARD AND PAINFUL smashed against his ribs. Luis shook his head and opened his eyes. He could make out a man dressed in blue overalls kicking him.

"Get out of here you goddamned bum!" He emphasized his words with another kick.

Camioneto had stood up at the noise. The man in blue kept kicking Luis who was trying to shield himself with his hands. Through the door of the freight car streamed a pale ray of sunlight. The car was stopped at some station. There were adobe houses, people busy about their business. What had happened? But this wasn't exactly the time to find out —he had to help Luis who was still taking a beating from this brute.

He was a giant with great shoulders and no neck. He wore a cloth cap with a visor turned up. Evidently he didn't realize that Luis had a friend with him and that the friend was about to go into action.

In situations like this one, anything was fair: If I only had a knife. Sure, there were two of them — but the railroad man could smash both of them with only one hand. Camioneto crept up behind him and before he had time to duck he crashed a fist like a sledgehammer a little below the man's left ear. For a second the man remained as though paralyzed. Camioneto let go another in exactly the same place. He cursed as he felt the bones in his hand crack. The giant swayed and then pitched forward to his knees as though made of lead.

"Beat it!" Camioneto managed to shout as he leaped from the boxcar.

He had run a hundred yards down a stony, manure-laden side street before he looked to see if Luis was following him. He slowed down to let Luis catch up, then together, sweating and panting, they continued their flight.

Ten minutes later when they stopped to rest under a tree a long way from the station, Luis began to complain of the pain in his shoulder. Camioneto examined him rapidly and diagnosed it as nothing serious, just badly bruised.

"What I don't get," he said, taking deep welcome breaths, "is why that rotten boxcar got cut off here."

Luis tucked in his shirttails and kneaded his painful shoulder.

"And where the devil is here? What's this place called?"

Camioneto discovered his right hand was swollen from the blows.

"Whatever it's called we'll find out soon enough."

Outside the Sanctuary of the Child God of the Silver-smiths, a little wayside church decorated with silver and gold, a rancher informed them that the town they saw in the distance was Fresnillo, in the state of Zacatecas.

When they walked into the town Camioneto thought they'd better take stock of their financial situation.

"We've still got a lot," said Luis.

"Then let's find a place to flop."

They wandered around for an hour. Fresnillo was a clean city and on one corner they came across a sign that announced:

BOARDINGHOUSE
ROOMS FROM ONE PESO

"This looks all right," said Camioneto.

They went in without knocking, into a big room with a mahogany table in the center which must have been the dining room.

"Good morning," called Camioneto.

They could hear a woman singing. From somewhere, presumably the patio, there came the sound of birds. Pancho repeated his greeting.

"Good morning — "

The singing voice stopped. They heard footsteps. In the doorway there appeared a tall woman. She was about forty, with reddish hair. She held a broom in her hand. She scrutinized them, smiling.

"What can I do for you?"

"We'd like to see the Señora — about a room."

"I'm the Señora."

She'd stepped closer to them now, and she kept studying them, still smiling. Camioneto assumed a formal air.

"We would like a room, señora, with two beds."

The woman motioned with her head for them to follow her. "I have some nice back ones." They went upstairs and passed through several rooms with high ceilings and bare walls. She opened the door of a bedroom.

"This is it. Come in."

They went in. It was a big room, practically empty. Just a double bed and a bureau. In the corner, a basin. Camioneto and Luis looked at each other.

"You see," said Luis, "we wanted two beds."

"It's the only free one I have. With the fair on we have a lot of guests."

It wasn't great but it was better than nothing. They tried out the bed for give and stuck their heads out the window, from which they could see part of the cobbled street below. The closet smelled of a combination of dust and disinfectant. The floor was of red tiles. The woman waited for them to decide.

"Señora," Camioneto felt her out diplomatically, "how much do you think this might cost us?"

"With or without food?"

"With food."

She did some figuring. These were two nice boys, especially the younger one, the brown-haired one with the green eyes. They seemed decent, polite and relatively clean. Of course they didn't have any luggage except the bundle and of course they were dressed rather shabbily and a little dusty —

"Look, señora, we're down on our luck a bit. We'll only be here a couple of days. We're toreros and — "

She opened her eyes wide. She put the broom aside and sat down on the edge of the bed. In her face was an expression of tenderness.

"Toreros?"

"Yes. We just came in town."

"How I like toreros!" she said. "You've come in for the priest's corrida?"

The toreros glanced at each other. So the good father was organizing a corrida?

"Yes, señora," said Luis. "That's why we're here."

"As you must know, señora," said Camioneto, trying to wrap it up, "we're a little short now but after the fight — "

She got up, her low neckline revealing her large white breasts as she did. At close range she was a rather appetizing woman, a little on the fleshy side but still good-looking. When she talked or smiled she showed a set of perfect white teeth. Her brown eyes sparkled with a certain natural flirtatiousness. Her hips were full and the solid thighs must be as ivory white as her neck and legs.

"If you are toreros, that's different. I like brave people."

"Thank you, señora."

"Stay for now. When you collect you can pay me."

She turned to smile at them from the hallway. She glanced at Luis with her dancing eyes.

"Want to eat? I'll fix something up."

"Fine, señora."

The woman prepared a luncheon which, in Camioneto's opinion, would raise a dead man: roast meat, eggs, beans, milk, coffee, all fixed with her own hands. While they ate she told them that she was the wife of a railroad switchman who spent three days of every week on the road, that her husband was mean and drunk and made her life miserable.

"Imagine," she sighed, looking deeply at Luis, "how lonely I get to feeling. He's either working or drunk. A lady alone here with so many temptations, she has to be a saint not to give in. Although there are times when — "

She didn't finish and lowered her eyes. Luis felt a little embarrassed for her, without knowing why. He'd just as soon not have her go on. A silence descended. She went on.

"There are times" — she picked up the sentence where she had left it — "when one isn't lacking in the opportunity nor the desire, right?"

"I guess so," Luis conceded.

"My old man doesn't understand. I know he's got a woman in Aguascalientes and another in Durango. I don't say anything because he's liable to kill me."

"Would he go that far?" said Camioneto.

"When he gets the wine in his brain he's bad. Understand? He's only got one arm, the left one, and he's got a steel hook on the stump, like they hang meat on in a butcher shop. When he gets mad" — she shuddered — "he always says he's going to lace it into me like a sewing machine."

After the meal they went to look for the priest. He wasn't in the church but the sacristan said they could find him at home. As they went, Luis was thinking about the woman and what she was hinting at. He felt some sympathy for her and also some attraction.

"Poor old biddy, eh?" he said suddenly.

Camioneto shrugged.

"They're all the same. They're all looking for a little."

"Maybe you're right."

The priest's house was large with a well-kept garden. A young girl, dressed in black, motioned them to step inside. They sat out on the little stone fountain. Soon they saw a rotund dark cassock coming down the hall. They went to meet him. The priest held out his hand for them to kiss.

"What can I do for you, lads?"

Camioneto led off bravely.

"Father, we're toreros, and we've come from Aguascalientes to bring you a message from Father Domínguez. You know him, of course."

The priest was surprised. Camioneto was very serene as he

glanced at Luis who looked even more surprised. The priest tried to remember who this Father Domínguez was.

"I believe so," he replied uncertainly.

"Well then," Camioneto replied, "Father Domínguez, who is a good friend of ours, has spoken a great deal about you, telling us that you know more about bullfighting than any priest in Zacatecas."

The priest smiled and swelled a little. He linked his fingers together and rested them on his fat stomach.

"I like the corridas," he conceded. "Yes, I do."

"Olé for the good aficionados!" Camioneto said, giving him a pat. "Well, Father Domínguez says to me a couple days ago, go to Fresnillo and tell his Excellency the priest there that I send regards and that I'd sure appreciate it if he'd let you fight in the corrida he's organizing. Those were his words. And here we are to deliver the message."

"The thing is," said the priest after clearing his throat, "I've already given my word to the toreros who are coming for the fight. I've even sent them their trip money to San Luis Potosí."

"That doesn't matter, Father. The matador here is going to fight free for you. And we can also help you with the advertising and ticket selling. And just how many toreros are you going to bring?"

"Two, since I only have four Ibarra bulls."

"How does this strike you then — we'll make a combination."

"How?" said the priest, a little interested now.

"Four bulls are coming. You got two toreros, and Luis makes three. Each of your boys fights a bull, then Luis the third one. The one who puts up the best fight gets to fight the fourth bull."

The priest thought about this for a minute. It wasn't bad.

Knowing that they'd see three fighters would excite the public more than if just two were announced. Not only that, with three of them competing for the last bull they'd all try their best. To include this boy on the program wouldn't cost any more.

"What do you say, Father?"

"Well," he said, "I think it's a good idea. Yes, I do."

The priest didn't know much about getting a corrida together. As a matter of fact this was his first experience. It was already Thursday and there still weren't any posters, or tickets or anything. The only sure thing was the bulls, which had been in the bull ring corral for almost a month. The priest showed just how green he was in these matters by having sent trip money to two unknown novilleros who lived in San Luis Potosí. Sure as fate, thought Camioneto, they'd keep the money and not bother to come and fight. All the better for Luis.

They convinced the priest that time was of the essence and that they had to get the publicity going. He brought them into his office and from a cedar chest he took a dozen rolls of change and he gave it to them to buy paints and canvas. They spent the rest of the afternoon painting the poster with large letters, featuring, naturally, the name of Luis Ortega, killer of novillo-bulls from the City of Mexico.

"The beauty of it is," Camioneto remarked as he admired his work, "that even a blind man could read your name."

It was the first time in his life that Luis had seen his name announced and it caused unexplainable emotion inside him. Luis Ortega, Matador de Novillos! It sounded so pretty. And it looked prettier. The poster would be hung in the square so nobody could miss it. After Sunday everyone would be talking about that name, because the person who owned it was out to justify its being in larger letters than the others on the poster.

The priest liked the poster fine and he gave them a couple of pesos to go get something to eat. Camioneto tendered a detailed report of the afternoon's activities.

"The printer, Father, he says he'll have the tickets ready on Saturday. They hadn't fed the bulls since yesterday, but I had them given some hay on your orders. Tomorrow early we're going to work out in the ring and at noon we'll be ready for your orders of the day."

The priest smiled with appreciation.

"Thank you, my sons."

They said goodbye and went back to the boardinghouse. The Señora was preparing dinner. They went to keep her company in the kitchen and told her that the priest was going to give them one hundred pesos for Sunday's performance. After stuffing themselves, they sat around the dining table chatting for several hours. The rest of the boarders were already in their rooms sleeping. The woman was animated, almost gay.

"When's your husband come back?" asked Camioneto.

"Uy! Not for three days. He got put on extra duty."

At ten Camioneto got up, yawning. It had been a long time since he'd eaten so much, and in succession. He felt heavy and sleepy and guessed he'd go up to bed.

"Let's go, Matador."

Talking about bullfighting with this woman who didn't know anything about the subject, but who knew how to listen attentively, Luis hadn't felt tired yet. He shook his head.

"Wait a while. Or go on up, and I'll be up in a minute."

"All right." Camioneto shook his shoulders. "But make it soon. Big day tomorrow."

When they were alone the woman brought more coffee and out of a cupboard she brought a bottle of Madero rum.

"Little drink?"

"No thanks, I never drink."

"Come on. Just one with your coffee."

Luis gave in. The coffee with the rum had a bitter taste. He had a sip and then lit another cigarette. The woman thought there was a little too much light in the room and she turned the lamp out. They sat there in the dark. Luis kept talking. From time to time he heard the sound of the bottle being tipped up. She had moved over closer to him.

"I like you," she said.

Instinctively Luis moved his chair over. One of the woman's hands rested on his thigh. The hand began to press against him. Luis's heart started beating harder. His mouth got like blotting paper.

"I like you a lot, torero," she said.

Her breath was alcoholic. Ortega felt her mouth very near. He wanted to get up. She prevented him. What her hand was doing under his pants was beginning to be very pleasant. The woman was aflame now. In the darkness she was moaning and panting and rubbing her full body up against Luis's. Suddenly, with an animal desire, he sought her lips. He didn't care whether they made any noise or not now. The boy's fingers explored the woman's white flesh. She stood up.

"Let's go to my room."

They went up hurriedly. The woman was breathing like a wounded animal. He pushed her down on the bed. When he took off her clothes Luis breathed in the good salty odor of fresh sweat.

31

AT SEVEN, CAMIONETO SHOOK HIM. "LATE, get moving."

Luis grunted for him to let him sleep. His legs felt weak and his kidneys hurt him. Lordy, what a party, he thought. Everything smelled of woman, even his face. When he had left her room at six his head was spinning. He'd opened the door to his room and slipped in cautiously so as not to awaken Camioneto. He'd lain down, done in.

Surely it hadn't been more than a minute when Camioneto woke him up.

He kept shaking him.

"Get up, you lazy bastard."

So that his friend wouldn't see the shape he was in he got up. While he washed his face and hands he tried to reconstruct what had happened from the time Camioneto had left him with the woman. Now he felt embarrassed to see her. How would she treat him after what had happened?

Camioneto opened the door.

"Step on it. See you downstairs."

He felt better when he was left alone. He got dressed slowly. The woman had a white, soft, smooth body that seared a person. Neither he nor she had closed their eyes until dawn. She never seemed to get enough.

When he looked in the mirror, with his comb in his hand, Luis found that he was very pale. He massaged the back of his neck, he rubbed his eyes, he slicked down his hair. When

he went down to the dining room the Señora greeted him
with a big smile.

"Good morning, Luisito!"

With his eyes lowered he murmured: "Morning, señora."

He listlessly ate his eggs and barely touched the coffee. He
was sagging from lack of sleep. She put one of her hands on
his shoulders and said to Camioneto: "Tell him to eat, so he'll
be ready for the bulls."

They were on their way out when she came up to them.
"Luisito, may I talk to you a moment?"

Coloring, Luis glanced at Camioneto and then at the woman.
She smiled warmly.

"Yes, señora?"

She put off Camioneto who had stopped to wait for Luis.

"I'll send him right along. Go ahead if you want — "

When Camioneto had left, the woman ran her hand over
Luis's head.

"Why so serious, Luisito?"

He raised his face. "I'm not serious," he stammered.

"You hardly spoke at breakfast."

"I . . . I . . ."

The big woman took him by the waist. Once again the
desire that Luis thought had been quenched forever began to
ignite inside his body. They glanced at each other. She gave
him a little shove towards the stairs.

"Were you happy last night?"

"Yes," he admitted, coloring.

"Want to be again?"

He preferred not to answer. But they went up to her room.
Luis looked around. On the bureau was the photo of a man
with a railroad cap on. He picked it up.

"My husband," she explained.

The man had the look of a wild animal in his dark eyes

His jaws were powerful and his mouth just a thin line. He put down the photo and turned around. The woman had taken off her clothes. She undid the sash that held up his trousers.

"Hurry," he said, "he's waiting for me."

Once stretched out on the bed his haste seemed to disappear completely. Camioneto and the world could wait. Everything except this ivory-pale woman.

"Stay with me!" she moaned.

"I can't —

"Stay. My husband's always away — there won't be any danger."

"Sure. But I can't."

"I'll give you whatever you want."

"It's not that — "

For an instant hate blazed in the woman's brown pupils. Then she sunk her white teeth into Luis's shoulder. The pain shot through his body. Automatically he pulled back like a bat and lashed out at her.

"More," she cried when the blow struck her, "more!"

Carried away, he kept striking her face.

"Harder, harder!"

And suddenly a sensation infinitely superior to that of rage or pain, something without shape or form, fleeting and terrible and wonderful, crushed the very marrow of their bodies. Then everything became dark and serene and warm.

32

THEY WERE COMING DOWN THE STAIRS, ARMS around each other's waist, when the woman's body went rigid and her smiling face went pale with terror.

"What's wrong?" he asked, trembling.

She merely held out her hand, pointing to the man coming up. Luis knew instantly who he was and he felt his blood sink down to his tennis shoes. The man came up slowly, stamping his black boots heavily on each step. He was wearing a blue cap, stiff with grease, and on the right forearm there glistened a steel hook that he held up when he saw them.

"Him," the woman whispered, terrified.

The man stopped on the first landing. He smiled, shaking his head with an expression that showed he had always expected what his eyes now gazed on. Luis let go of the woman who had remained frozen. The saliva dried in his mouth and his hands were wet with sweat. The hook, like a great steel finger, rested on the banister. It was like a bull's horn hooking into the barrera fence.

"What's new, old lady?" rasped the man.

He seemed to be very calm, with his cruel, smiling mouth "Caught you in the act, right?"

She whispered: "Run for it, Luis — "

But what the devil could he do? The staircase was blocked by the man. Going back up the stairs was useless since he'd just come after him and trap him. To stay there was worse the man was starting up again. The idea of trying to fight him was insanity. There was nothing to do but run, retreat, if not with dignity at least with speed. He glanced down over the banister. He'd have to jump ten feet. The man, guessing the boy's intention, backed up three steps. The woman stayed absolutely still, very pale. The apple color of her face had gone. She knew what would happen. When her husband went calm and silent like this, with the hook in readiness, somebody always bled.

She glanced at the young torero. His boyish face was drawn with fear.

The man jabbed the sharp hook point into the banister and repeated his greeting.

"What's new, old lady? Surprise you?"

"Please" — she began and then her mouth just worked helplessly.

Luis decided to chance it at that moment. Grabbing the banister with both hands he leaped over it, agilely, like a torero going over the fence. The other man saw him and quickly ran down the stairs. Luis felt the floor smack the soles of his feet. It was like fleeing from a bull. He scrambled up, but lost his footing and went down to his knees. He lurched to his feet and tried to lunge away. The man was near enough to reach out and swing his mutilated arm, slashing down with the hook. Luis felt a great searing pain that ripped from his neck to his waist, and he heard the tearing of his shirt.

The woman screamed.

"Don't kill him!"

Luis whirled, stunned. The man with the hook was about to hurl himself upon him to run him through like a beetle. For a fraction of a second the light glanced off the hook as it was raised high. Luis ducked automatically, the blow missed him, and he spun and lunged for the door.

Gasping for breath, dripping sweat from every pore, he ran without stopping for several blocks. He must have had an expression of great terror on his face because people in th street turned to look at him. When he knew he was safe, h slowed down. Finally he stopped, choking for breath, lean ing up against a corner, feeling broken inside. His leg wobbled as though they didn't belong to him. He wante to spit but nothing came out of his mouth. In front of him on the other side of the street, he saw the poster with his nam and under it: "The bravest novillero in the world."

He took a deep breath and ran his hand over his back When he touched it he knew he'd got it. He looked at hi fingers, streaked with blood. Couldn't be more than a scratch but God how it hurt. He thought of Camioneto. He'd hav been waiting in the plaza for a long time. On legs of gelati he staggered on to look for him.

The plaza was where Camioneto was. When he saw Lui come up, pale and beaten, he shook him.

"What's happened to you?"

"Nothing," he said and sagged down on a bench.

Camioneto saw the torn and bloody shirt and the swea pouring from the boy's neck.

"Spit it out — what happened?"

"Somebody tried to skin me."

"Why? Where?"

Luis took some time before answering. "Back there, at th house."

"And why?"

"How should I know?"

Camioneto wasn't satisfied with the explanation. He pushe Luis's head forward so that he could examine the wound. H whistled when he saw it.

"Nice little gash you're sporting. Luckily it's just a ri If the knife had gone in just a little more, you'd be a gone now."

"Wasn't a knife."

"What then?"

"A hook."

"Ah!" Camioneto faced Luis. "All right, the truth."

"It was the husband," Luis began slowly. He didn't take his eyes off the ground. "Coming out of the room when he arrived."

"Her room?"

"Yes."

"I figured."

"I tried to run for it but he nailed me."

"If he catches you, God. He'll butcher you."

"So now what?" said Luis anxiously.

"All we can do is beat it," he said.

"But where?"

In view of what had happened they could not stay for the night on Sunday. The man with the hook would track Luis down and try to finish the job he'd begun. Camioneto chewed on the nail of one thumb. He spat between his feet and then set to thinking, his jaw resting between his hands.

"Weren't we going to Noria del Ojo? Well, let's go there."

There was a silence. The rip down his back pained him, but more painful was the idea of having to leave Fresnillo without having been able to perform after having already been advertised. Finally Luis spoke.

"Sorry, mano."

"That's all right, Luis. But Jesus, man, you're stupid."

"I know," said Luis.

"You're always getting messed up in somebody's bloomers. Why don't you just realize that women are poison for us?"

"Hell, I didn't want to," Luis protested.

"You didn't want to what? Sleep with her?"

"Honest."

"Hah! Sure it's hard to say no. But you got to learn what's good for you and what isn't, and right now women aren't."

"Sure, Pancho," Luis admitted humbly.

33

THEY WALKED ALL AFTERNOON UNDER A fierce sun. The long wound pained Luis, but he didn't complain once. At sundown they came to a village, sad and brown. They learned that it was Sombrerete.

At a gasoline pump there was a truck getting its tank filled. Bent over the motor a man was adjusting the oil level. They went up to him.

"Señor," Camioneto began.

The man turned around. He was short, young, with a mass of hair curling out of his shirt front. He wiped off his hands with a rag.

"What's up?"

"Can you give us a lift?"

The driver swung up into the cab. He started up the motor, threw in the clutch, and as he shifted into low he signaled them to climb up.

They scrambled up and made themselves comfortable in the back part of the truck. Through the little window they could see the nape of the driver's neck. Soon the truck was speeding along at fifty down a highway full of bumps and dust.

In the darkness of the night the truck pulled up. The tires skidded, the brakes squealed, there was a shaking, and then everything stopped.

"Hey," said Luis. "Wake up."

"Let me sleep," Camioneto mumbled.

"Let's find out what happened."

Luis threw aside the cape that was covering him. A cold wind lashed his face when he stuck it up over the driver's cab. His back didn't hurt much now. The night was very quiet. He looked around. The India ink of the night obscured everything, truck, people, everything. Camioneto kept on dozing. Luis could see nothing. But he could hear two voices, the rough one of the driver and another. Then the order: "Climb on up."

He saw the form of someone coming around to the end of the truck. Something white was tossed in and lit at Luis's feet. Two hands gripped the top board of the back of the truck. Then a cap appeared, a blur of a face, and a slim body. The driver started off in a series of jerks. The newcomer stopped when he saw Luis's outline.

"Hi," he greeted.

"Hi," said Luis.

The stranger knelt to gather up his bundle and then made himself comfortable in a free corner. It was unprotected and windy there. He remained still for a few minutes, as though not even alive, his identity hidden by the shadows. There was a slight noise as though the newcomer was trying to cover himself up with a blanket or something.

Leaning back against the driver's cabin, Luis let himself slide down until he was seated. His eyes tried to pierce the gloom. The new man didn't even move. Luis took out a package of cigarettes, stuck one in his mouth, and held out the package.

"Smoke?"

"No," said the other.

"Go on. Good for the cold."

"All right."

A hand came out and took one of the cigarettes. Luis lit his. The wind blew out the flame instantly. The other waited. Luis reached out his cigarette for him to get a light off it.

They smoked without speaking for a while. Luis tried to guess what his guest was like. Seemed to be a youth, small and very young.

"What's new?" Luis asked to start off.

"Nothing."

"Where you coming from?"

"Long ways away."

"Ah."

"And you?"

"From Fresnillo."

"I was there last week."

"What do you do?"

"Torero."

"What?" Luis pricked up his ears.

"Torero. And you?"

"We're in the same business."

"What's your name?"

"Luis Ortega."

"Me — Mario Valente."

"Never heard of you."

Mario took a hard pull on his cigarette.

"You will."

Luis poked Camioneto in the ribs. He grunted to be left alone.

"This guy here is a torero."

"Congratulations," mumbled Camioneto.

"Us," Luis bragged, "we're going up to train on the small cows up at the ranch at Noria del Ojo."

"Me too."

"Been there ever?"

"No. But the rancher is a good guy, I know that much."

Mario shivered when a blast of freezing air hit him as they rounded a corner. Luis moved over to make room.

"Move in closer here. The cold doesn't hit you so much."

"No, thanks. I'm fine."

"Come on over," Luis insisted.

Mario came over, and they sat next to each other. Hunched up in a ball, Camioneto snored on shamelessly. From time to time he'd mutter a curse as the truck hit a bump. Then back to sleep.

"Been with the bulls long?" Luis asked.

"A year."

"Me, about two now."

The conversation lagged a bit. Both of them had their eyes half closed with sleep. Silent gaps grew longer each time. Soon nobody spoke any more.

34

WITH HIS FOOT ON THE RUNNING BOARD, THE driver banged with the flat of his hand on the tin roof of the protected part of the back of the truck.

"Get up, kids!"

They woke up with a start. Mario kept sleeping, his head resting on Luis's chest. When Camioneto saw him he let out a laugh.

"And where'd the kid come from?"

"He's been out in the wars — climbed up last night."

The driver gestured impatiently. "Don't talk so much and get going. Noria del Ojo is near here."

"What's this place called?"

"Puanas."

Mario kept leaning his head on Luis who woke him up with a jab of his elbow.

"On your feet, mano. Fun's fun but we got to get going."

It had dawned. Between the distant profile of the mountains and the dark bowl of sky, a luminous gap was growing wider and wider by the minute. It was still chilly. The three toreros jumped down to the road. Luis studied Mario as he did his cape in his bundle. The boy's face, pale, sensitive and beardless, made a good impression on him. He had amazing eyes.

When the truck turned off, they waved. In front of them stretched the dusty highway. A lone tree writhed its trunk in front of the lonely landscape. Another road went off to the side.

Without thinking too much about it, Camioneto decided this must be the one to Noria del Ojo.

"If it isn't, what does it matter?"

They walked along for almost an hour without saying anything. They felt hungry. Everything around them was gray, dry, dusty. The dust scraped their throats and sandpapered their eyes. Where the hell was this damned ranch of Noria del Ojo? They made wild guesses, since none of them had been there they hadn't the slightest idea how far it was.

"Hey," Luis whispered. "What do you think of this guy?"

Mario was walking ahead a few steps at this moment. Camioneto narrowed his eyes to study him better even if it were just from behind.

"He's just a kid."

"Have you seen his eyes?"

"No, what's wrong with them?"

"Nothing, they're just — " Luis swallowed. "They're good-looking."

A great laugh came from Camioneto. He laughed till the tears came to his eyes. Mario turned his face and smiled too, without knowing at what. Luis went serious.

"Shut up, Camioneto."

He stopped laughing as quickly as he'd started. "You know about the guy and the mule — how after he'd been off in the wilds for three months without seeing a woman how pretty he thought the mule was getting — that's you!"

Luis colored and protested.

"No, I was just saying take a look at them and you'll see what I mean."

"Nothing doing, mano. I might start to like them. And you know if you try that stuff it means seven years' bad luck!"

They came to the edge of a dam and there they sat down for a rest. The sun was high over them, baking their heads and bodies. The hot sweat ran down their necks. The wound down his back began to itch Luis badly.

"Lord, how far is this place?" Camioneto panted, mopping his brow.

Luis stood up and took off his shirt.

"Let's take a dip."

It seemed like a good idea to Camioneto.

"Right." He stripped down like Luis.

Luis waded out naked in the clear, clean water up to his knees. He called to Mario: "Come on, kid. It's fine."

He shook his head, looking away uninterestedly.

"Don't feel like it."

"Come on, boy, it'll really pep you up."

When he declined again, Camioneto said: "Hell, if he doesn't want to, skip it."

The water was fine. In that devilish heat it gave them a wonderful refreshing surge of life, invigorating their muscles and quenching the thirst of their parched skins.

"Camioneto —" Luis swam over to his friend, his feet

splashing. "Just got an idea —" He shook his head like a wet dog.

"What now?"

"About him —" he pointed over at Mario.

"What about him?"

"Let's give him a scare. I think he's a fairy. Last night sleeping on me and now he tries not to look at us naked and the way he won't come swimming with us."

Camioneto looked over at Mario. He was sitting on the side of the dam resting his chin on his knees and never looking over at them.

"Look, we'll both get out at the same time, we'll strip the bastard and then chuck him in."

They got out of the water silently and then, howling like savages they flung themselves on Mario. He turned as he heard the din. His eyes flashed with panic. He tried to get up but it was too late. The other two were on him. Valente tried to defend himself with kicks and scratches, but he was weak. The three bodies rolled over the soft ground and down the bank, Luis and Camioneto laughing and Mario groaning with an impotent fury. Finally Mario was stretched out on his back, and Luis sat on his stomach holding both the boy's wrists in his left hand. Then he ordered Camioneto: "Grab his feet."

When Mario was completely helpless, Luis began to unbutton his shirt. The boy made one last struggle. With tears in his eyes he cried: "Let me up, you cowardly bastard!"

Luis smiled.

"You hear, Camioneto? He says" — Luis mimicked a falsetto — " 'Let me up, you nasty fellow!' "

"Strip him, for Christ's sake."

Impatient because the buttons wouldn't come loose, Luis grabbed the shirt with both hands and ripped it open.

He gasped and pulled back, as though he'd seen a rattle-snake. He went pale, then red. Mario Valente was crying. Ortega stayed sitting on the victim, his arms limply hanging at his sides.

"What the hell's got into you?" said Camioneto, who was tired of holding Mario's feet.

Luis got up. Mario watched him, shyly, still moaning.

Camioneto stood up too.

"Well what's happened?"

Luis could only point.

"It's — it's — " he stammered — "a woman."

"What?"

"I — I saw it. Tits — tits like a woman's."

Woman! Luis was crazy. Camioneto'd see for himself. He flung himself on Mario, dug his fingers in his neck with one hand to keep him quiet, while the other opened up the shirt.

What his eyes took in and what he felt with his fingers left no doubt. Those solid, pink-nippled protuberances were breasts, and Mario was a woman. He felt them again for good measure.

Camioneto felt a hand smack his shoulder, almost knocking him over backwards. When he straightened up he saw Luis in front of him glaring angrily.

"Leave her," said Luis firmly. "Leave her alone!"

35

THEY ARRIVED AT NORIA DEL OJO BY MID-afternoon. The low building was gray and still, very different from the haciendas in the center of the country. They called out several times to see if there was anyone around. Silence and silence echoed was their answer. Their steps resounded strangely in the vast loneliness. Not even dogs, usually everywhere in the country, came to bark at them.

They walked around the outside wall whose gate was locked. The first indication that Noria del Ojo wasn't a ghost ranch was a bovine bellow. This encouraged them. Their steps quickened and upon coming around a corner they found themselves facing a corral where a bull was feeding. But not an ordinary stable bull. This one was a big black beautiful creature with a glistening coat and fine conformation.

"It must be the seed bull," said Luis admiringly when they stopped to look at it.

Camioneto slung the cape bundle down next to the corral.

"Wait here. I'm going to see if there isn't someone around."

When he had limped away, Luis could smile openly at Mario Valente who had stayed a few steps behind. Since the happening at the reservoir they hadn't exchanged a word. The girl, her buttonless shirt knotted at the waist, had kept several feet behind them all the way. From time to time, when Camioneto wasn't noticing, Luis would cast furtive glances at her in an attempt to be nice.

A disconcerting thing had been working inside Luis. From the moment he'd discovered she was a girl he had felt a warm and tender and deep feeling for her. It was a protective feeling. He began to feel anxiety for what could happen to her traveling with them like this, for what could have happened before they'd met her. Who was she, where had she come from and why had she chosen this wretched, hungry, nomadic way of life?

Now for the first time they were alone. He smiled at her again. On Mario's face there were still traces of resentment against him. Seeing her so serious and quiet, Luis tried to imagine how she'd be dressed as a woman, how her hair would fall down over her shoulders if she'd let it out of the prison of her grubby cap.

"Listen," he said, and he couldn't go on because he couldn't find the right words.

She looked straight at him. Almost without moving her lips she said: "Listen what?"

"I'm sorry — about this morning."

"That's all right," the girl said offhandedly.

Luis offered her a cigarette, which she accepted. In order to light it he went over and sat by her.

"See," he went on, "I didn't know you were female."

"I wasn't broadcasting it."

Thoughtfully, Luis drew the smoke from his cigarette into his lungs.

"I just don't get it."

"What?"

"What are you — a female — what are you doing in the wars?"

"Is that so strange? You mean there aren't any other girl bullfighters?"

"Sure, but not the way you're doing it."

"I like the way I'm doing it."

"Sure, but why man's clothes, why all alone?"

"It's a long story. Someday I'll tell you."

Luis had another question and he tried it several ways mentally to find one that wouldn't get her mad.

"And — " he began without looking at her, "and nothing's ever happened to you?"

"What do you mean?"

"I mean — " Lord, it was ticklish — "I mean, since you're a girl, hasn't anyone ever — ever — "

She laughed for the first time. It was a pleasant laugh.

"Oh, you mean that. No, nothing's ever happened to me
And nothing will until I decide when and with whom."

"Naturally."

"Look, I might as well tell you my long sad story once and
for all. My stepfather was chasing me around the house all
the time. Maybe it seems strange but that's the way it was.
One day a troupe of girl bullfighters came into our village.
liked the idea, I spoke to the boss, he said fine, and I took off
with them at dawn."

"And your family?"

"My mother doesn't matter and my stepfather's a heel.
traveled all over the place. The day they let me make my
first cape pass I got my first tossing, but I came through all
right. There were three toreras in the troupe. One was the
mistress of the boss and the other two girls — well, they had
an arrangement."

"Ah."

"One night things got rough after we'd performed at the
fair in Los Altos. The boss got drunk and tried to make love
to me. I grabbed a puntilla knife and when he came at me
cut him up a bit. Since then I've preferred to go it alone."

"And how long have you been traveling as a man?"

She pressed her cigarette out on the corral logs. She blew
out smoke, spat out of one side of her mouth in an attempt at
a manly gesture, and wiped her lips with her shirt sleeve.

"Ever since I found out they were all trying to get in me,"
she said. "They'd laugh at me when I'd beg to be allowed to
fight and they'd say I'd do much better going to bed with
them. I said, 'I'll do that when I feel like it and with someone
I like.'"

"Well said." Luis was already making his plans.

"So I cut off my hair and said goodbye to skirts and I'd
still be a man if it hadn't been for your bright little idea."

Luis was amused by her, so much so that he'd almost forgotten how hungry he was.

"Take off your cap," he said.

Surprised, she looked at him for a second. But then she obeyed. Luis could see that she was not only pretty, but very pretty. Her hair, parted like a man's, was copper colored and made her delicate features stand out.

"You're pretty," he said softly.

The girl lowered her eyes. Nobody had ever said anything so tenderly to her before. She felt grateful to Luis. She'd never seen a young torero be gentle before.

"You think I'm pretty?"

"Yes," said Luis, reddening, "very pretty. How old are you?"

"Eighteen."

Then Luis laughed. She looked up, frowning and wary again. "What's so damned funny?"

"I don't even know your name — your woman's name."

She laughed too. Then she said,

"María — María Valente."

Camioneto appeared as they were lighting the second cigarette.

"Put them out and come on. The rancher's over there."

They followed him quickly. At the far end of the corrals were piled great quantities of ears of corn, yellow and stinking as they rotted in the sun.

A big-shouldered man was sitting on an incredibly small stool stripping the corn. Three silent, clay-colored workers helped him, barely glancing up as the young toreros came up to them.

"Señor Rancher," Camioneto began.

He of the giant shoulders looked up for a moment, and then went back to his task. "What do you want, boys?"

"Señor —" They all took a step forward. "We're toreros and we've just arrived."

"From where?"

"From Fresnillo. And everyone told us that the Noria del Ojo is a right place and that you'd let us fight some heifers."

The rancher threw the kernelless ear to one side and took up a fresh one in his great hand. His fingers made the kernels fly in yellow streams as he talked.

"So you want to fight."

"If we can."

"We got plenty to fight here. But first you got to work to earn the bravery you're going to cape out of the animals and to pay for what you're going to eat."

Camioneto's face fell. "Sure," he said.

"Strip that corn there and then we'll talk." He pointed to a giant pile of ears.

Within five minutes their fingers were raw and their kidneys aching. The afternoon sun burned them and their stomachs were growling for attention. Wiping the sweat off his face, Camioneto muttered: "Lord, how one suffers for art!"

36

THE RANCHER MOPPED HIS BALD HEAD WITH his bandanna.

"If you feel like it, we'll turn lose the seed bull for you."

"You bet we feel like it," said Luis, though his stomach contracted at the thought of that big animal.

"Soon as you finish then."

They'd been four days at Noria del Ojo now, working a lot, eating a little and dreaming more. In these past ninety-six hours, they had spoken of nothing but how great it would be when they'd be allowed to fight. When they finally finished the daily corn duty, they'd head straight for the little testing arena. Then they would unfold the capes and muletas and under the supervision of Camioneto, they'd begin to work out. María acted just like a man, never shirking when it was her turn to play the bull and charge at Luis. Camioneto treated her as though she were a man and spoke in his roughest language in front of her. Luis called him aside one night and asked him to hold it down in front of her, and Camioneto had answered that nothing he could possibly think of to say would shock her.

"No matter what you think," Luis had asked, "take it easier."

Camioneto had smiled. "You think she's a saint, don't you? She's just a tramp."

"You don't have any reason to say that."

"I know something about women, and I'm not mistaken. This one's no better than the rest."

"Why don't you like her?"

"Why should I?"

"She's a girl."

"That's the trouble."

"I don't see why?"

"I'm not blind. You should see your stupid face when she's around."

"And so?"

"The girl's a bum. She's just out for herself. You'll see. Women are poisonous for a torero, I keep telling you."

And that is all they said about María. Now she was the most excited and the most industrious as they worked hard to finish up the pile. It was noon and the sun was blazing. The boys were stripped to the waist. María hadn't even taken off her cap.

"While you finish up," said the rancher, "I'll tell them to get the bull ready to come in the ring."

"Sí, señor!"

When the last ear had been stripped, they ran to their room in the servants' quarters for their equipment. Luis and Camioneto cinched up their shirts and fitted the notched stick in the muletas. María wetted down the capes without asking for advice or help. Luis turned to look at her. He liked to sneak looks at her when she wasn't aware of it. There was something fascinating about her face, something soft but surly, something feminine yet fierce, something boyish yet little girlish too. Camioneto caught Luis's look.

"Pay attention to your business," Camioneto growled between his teeth.

They started down toward the ring, a small arena but complete with burladero shields, a toril gate, and a corral in back. Luis said to María under his breath: "You're not fighting, of course."

"And why not?"

"I mean the bull is so big and — "

María laughed. She put her small hand on Camioneto's shoulder. "Hey," she mocked. "Know what the matador here said? He doesn't want me to fight because the bull weighs a bit!"

Camioneto cast a withering glance at his friend. "And who are you to keep her from making a few passes at the animal? Let her if she wants."

Luis didn't answer. If something goes wrong, he thought, its goodbye for her. And he realized that suddenly, for some evil reason, he wanted something to go wrong.

The rancher was waiting for them in the ring. He had in

his hands a shabby cape covered with patches and almost as old as the capes of the toreos. As the man squeezed his bulk behind one of the burladero shields, Camioneto thought how funny it was going to be to see this fat body trying to execute any bullfighting maneuvers.

"Hey, Matías!" shouted the rancher.

One of the peons who had helped them strip corn showed his sombrero above the toril gate.

"At your service, patrón."

"Turn him out!"

The little gate was banged open and amidst a gray cloud of dust there appeared the bull's horns. How different he looked to them now, now that they were going to have to stand up to his savagery! While grazing in the corral he seemed so peaceful. Now it was different. Six years old with a short thick neck swollen with rage, his horns looked like twin death to Luis. The bull jabbed them viciously into the planks and then ran around the ring looking for something more interesting to hook. Finally he stopped in the center of the ring, arrogantly, his head up as he snuffed challengingly, his tail whipping his flanks.

Their heads barely showing from behind the burladero shield, the young toreros didn't take their eyes off the animal for a second. Luis's mouth was dry and bitter. He glanced over at María; she was pale and her chin trembled slightly.

Without looking at them, the owner said: "You — the brown-haired one — get out there!"

"Me?" said Luis, knowing he didn't mean him.

"No, the other boy."

"Sí, señor," said María starting out.

"As soon as I double him to see how he works, out you go."

María swallowed. Luis, frightened now, spoke up: "Not him, patrón — better me."

"Christ, didn't you hear me?" The man glared at Luis. "I said him first, then you. You'll get your turn."

In spite of his fatness, the man was agile. He went out towards the bull and when it charged, he swirled his cape out in front of its nose and jumped back out of the way. He held the cape by one corner and doubled the bull back in its tracks twice more, and then he ran behind a burladero.

"All right," he panted, "it's your bull!"

María got the cape firmly in her hands and ran out towards the bull. She cited fairly close to the boards. When the animal didn't charge, she shook the cape and took a few running steps out towards the middle, saying "Toro, ah — haaaaa . . ."

The animal lunged towards her. In the burladero, Luis's heart stopped beating. From the time the horns came even with the cape until they skimmed by her legs, a hundred years elapsed.

"Olé!!"

A joyous shout came from the rancher's lips as María kept caping the animal. What guts this young torero was showing!

Then, suddenly, as María tried to finish off the series with a half-verónica, the animal put on the brakes and jerked its head to the right. María was propelled up into the clear warm air, and like a rag puppet she spilled to the ground.

Instantly, Luis, Camioneto, and the rancher were in the ring running to save her. The bull had a horn under María's inert body and now it flung her into the air again. Luis had never suffered as he did in those moments. He felt his limbs go weak, mutinying. She was still there between the animal's front legs, instinctively covering her head with her arms.

"Toro!" the three shouted trying to distract the animal with their flashing capes. "Toro, toro!"

The rancher finally managed to lure the bull away from the girl's body and in a series of choppy passes he enticed it to the far side of the little arena. Luis ran to María. But she pushed him away as she lurched to her feet. She grabbed up the cape and without even looking at her torn clothing, without even feeling the pain in her body, with blood streaming from her mouth and one cheek, she went after the bull while tears of rage spilled from her eyes.

Luis tried to head off the bull's charge, but the owner shouted: "Leave him alone!"

María stopped and had time to shake the cape once to attract the animal's attention away from her body. As it bore down on her she fought the urge to run. Instead, she stood rock still, dropped her left hand onto her right hip, while the right hand described a circle which wrapped the cape around her in a perfect classic, Belmonte-type half-verónica as the animal sliced by. Then, arrogantly, her chin out, her shoulders squared, she turned her back and marched back to the burladero.

"Olé!" cheered the owner as he clapped the girl's shoulder with rough enthusiasm. "Oooléee for real guts!"

Luis's eyes were opened wide and he kept looking at her — bloody, covered with dirt, dripping with sweat. The owner had to shake him to get his attention.

"Now you, boy. And you better be good, because this fellow's left you a tough row to hoe."

Very tough indeed. The worst. As he got the muleta right in his hands and started out he thought of the terrible bravery of this girl. How many senior matadors, even, would have gone right back to the bull after that terrible beating? And to stand there like a post and execute that marvelous half-verónica! If he didn't want to listen to Camioneto jabber for months to come, if he didn't want to suffer taunts from the rancher and perhaps even from María herself, Luis had to put everything he had into this and win the contest. Other people who had seen him had said he could be as brave as a lion, that he ate the bulls alive. Fine, that's what other people said, but what did he himself say? He was going to find out in three steps, when he began to "cross" with the enemy. "First, a pair of punishing passes," he heard Camioneto call out, "and not a step backward!"

When he stopped two yards from the big bull, he saw that the muleta cape in his right hand was moving. It was not because of any breeze, but because of the fear in his body. He tried to swallow but his mouth was a desert. He took another step forward. The bull bellowed once. Then it charged, jerking its head from side to side dangerously as it lunged. It was a question of staying completely still the way María had done. Although he thought, in the brief moment he had to think as the animal bore down on him, that he was going to get tossed, Luis didn't step back. He barely moved the cloth, and, to his surprise, the bull took the lure and went by. Then, with one knee bent, he shoved the tip of the muleta out under the bull's off horn and finished up the wrenching "doubling" pass. This preparatory maneuver came off gracefully, smoothly, perfectly. He repeated it three more times, wrenching the animal around in its tracks each time, working out from the fence toward the center of the ring as he did.

There he stopped and straightened up confidently. The big seed bull was dominated, its gray tongue already hanging out of its mouth. Reaching out with one hand he took hold of the right horn, and, turning his head disdainfully, he looked over at his friends.

"Olé!"

"Now start passing him!" Camioneto shouted jubilantly.

And right there in that little piece of ground, Luis Ortega fought that immense brave animal which he had succeeded in dominating by guts alone, and he fought as he never before had done. He fought it feeling himself for the first time the priest of the divine rite, supreme god of the muleta, beginning and end of la fiesta brava. He fought as in a dream. That inexplicable emotion that sometimes can come to one when fighting a bull, that delight that no other physical pleasure can compete with, that magic, shining anguish, that drunkeness that blinds and transports — it was all his, completely selfishly his, as his muleta toyed with the bull and made it do whatever he willed.

When he finally staggered over to the fence, unseeing, unhearing, he knew that this was his destiny and that the bulls could never hurt him as long as he could find the will and the guts within himself to stand up to them. And he also understood how willingly one might exchange a life of hunger for a death of glory.

37

"LUIS," CALLED A VOICE WHICH HE RECOGnized immediately.

He was up on top of the thatched shed to the left of the little bull ring. The moonlight elongated his shadow and stretched it across the arena. He'd been there for some time — an hour, maybe two. He'd been thinking of things, making plans for the future, enjoying the aloneness. Camioneto would be sleeping, like the rest of them over there in the servants' quarters. María now appeared below him in the shadows. In the moonlight her face looked metallic, silver plated.

"Hola," he said. He extended his hand and helped her up.

"What are you doing?" she asked as she made herself comfortable next to him.

"Here — thinking."

"You know something." She lowered her head. "I haven't even thanked you for making that *quite*."

Luis tossed the unlit cigarette he'd been chewing into the empty ring. "It wasn't anything. You'd have done the same for me."

"Anyway, thanks."

After a pause, he said, "You fought well."

"Yes?"

"You really put your heart into it."

"It still hurts where he stepped on me. And my face is burning. Look."

She drew closer and held her face up to Luis. He took the girl's chin in his fingers. The skin felt fresh, firm, clean. He couldn't keep his eyes from slipping down to her neck that lost itself in the openness of the man's shirt she wore. He thought again of the happening by the reservoir and his mind again saw the small fine breasts.

"I'm going to have this on me for a least a week, I'll bet."

"Yes," he answered vaguely, taking his hand away.

"How ugly I'll be."

Luis took out some cigarettes and offered her one. She refused. He lit up and as he blew out the smoke, he studied her. She didn't look away. Luis noticed for the first time how full her lips were and how well formed.

"What a fight you put up," she said.

"You liked it?"

"You're a fine torero, Luis. You'll eat well off it, too."

"Ham and butter every day," he joked.

She stroked her thighs. Then cocking her head she asked: "You have a sweetheart in Mexico City?"

He pushed the hair back from his forehead. "No. And you?"

"I've never had one."

"Would you like to?"

"Depends."

"And nothing's ever happened to you?"

"No. I told you that."

For some time Luis had been thinking that it was high time something did happen to her. He seriously doubted her story about never having been with a man. It couldn't be. She wasn't a child and living the life she led it would be impossible. We'll find out, he thought to himself.

He stood up and jumped down. Then held out his hand for her. When she jumped down they stood very close for a moment. He felt the warmth of her breasts trembling under the shirt.

"How about a walk?"

"Fine," she said.

There was a path nearby and they took it. The air smelled sharply of fertilizer. In a remote field some bulls bellowed. They walked along silently. As they passed the last peon hut they found themselves in an open meadow. A hundred yards away was a tree whose silvery branches and leaves looked transparent in the light. María walked along slowly, head down, moving her hands like a child in time with her legs. Her shirt sleeve rolled up to her elbow brushed Luis's. Then their arms bumped and their fingers entwined.

"Let's go to the tree," he said simply.

"Whatever you wish." María's voice was barely audible.

As he had expected, there was hay under the tree. They sat down on it. He pushed her down gently. She didn't say anything. Leaning on his elbow, Luis stretched out next to her and kept looking at her. When she breathed, María's breasts moved under the shirt.

"I like you," he said softly.

She bent her head.

"I like you," he repeated.

"I like you, too."

Luis's head cast a shadow over her eyes and his lips sought hers. They were firm and stayed open as he kissed her. Luis sat halfway up, breathing hard.

"I kissed you."

"Yes. It was nice."

He grabbed her to him and as his teeth went hard against her lips, his hand slipped down the opening of her shirt. His fingers fumbled on the girl's breasts and she quivered.

"Do you want to?"

She nodded yes. It is time it happened, she thought. She was glad that the first was to be Luis. She wasn't sure why, but she was glad. But then she became suddenly afraid and confused and panicky. Luis was bending over her. She tried to push him away.

"Let me alone!" she cried suddenly, trying to get up.

He pinned her down by one shoulder and loosened the sash around her waist. María began to kick out. Luis looked at her slowly, tensely, with the quiet calm of the desire that had made the veins in his neck swell, that made him breathe with difficulty. He shook her once hard.

"Stop it," he said, holding up one hand, "or I'll hit you."

Now María didn't offer any more resistance. She closed her eyes and waited for him to do whatever he willed with her.

38

WHEN THEY WERE ALL ON HORSEBACK, THE
rancher shouted: "Let's go!"

For half an hour they galloped across the yellow fields. The
dusty heat got in their eyes and made their bodies sweat.
They were going to cut out three corridas of bulls to be
fought in the nearby village of Nombre de Dios at the fair.
The job was a punishing one under the ruthless sun which
parched the fields and made the dry plant life scream for relief. All morning they spent on the go, picking out the animals. The rancher was a fine horseman, as were his two over-
seers. Camioneto, Luis, and María were just along for the
ride.

By one o'clock, when the heat was smothering, they had
managed to round up twelve animals in one field. Standing
up in their stirrups the horsemen studied them from a distance.

The rancher mopped his bald head with his bandanna.

"Well now," he said to Luis, "I wonder which of these
animals you'll draw."

"I wonder," answered Luis, thoughtfully. He also had been
mentally picking and choosing two of those brave black bulls,
the two he might draw in the sorting. The rancher, after
having seen Luis with the big seed bull, had made plans for
him. He would arrange for him to fight in one of the novilladas of the fair, since he had great influence with the impresario.

"My bulls," he said, "are perfect for your style. Their
charge is smooth, but to get it out of them you really have to
work in close, wait out the charge, and gear them down."

Then something off there began happening. Two bulls had pulled away from the rest of the herd and began hooking at each other as they moved away. They were the two biggest and had given them the most trouble all morning.

The rancher spat out an oath, brought his quirt down on his pinto's flanks, and started off at a gallop to head them off.

"Come on," he shouted, "before they end up killing each other!"

The others galloped off after him, except for Luis and María. They watched the men disappear in clouds of dry dust towards the thick brush. Under the sun, under the clear blue sky they were left alone. They looked at each other silently. A little to the left was a shady tree. They rode to it and he dismounted. She did likewise. Without speaking, they lay down and put their arms around each other. He started to kiss her. María sat halfway up.

"They're coming."

Luis looked around. The countryside was deserted. Way off in the distance he could just barely hear the shouts of the vaqueros.

He laughed. "They won't be back for an hour."

María opened her arms and lay back peacefully. She closed her eyes and he began to kiss her. She liked the smell of this good-looking and nice boy. She was happy with him.

"No," said the girl as he began to undo the sash that served as her belt. "Not here."

"Yes," he said breathing on her cheek, "nobody will see us."

"They could come back."

"We'll do it before."

"It won't be nice now," she said, stroking his burning face with both hands. "Better tonight."

Luis opened her shirt and the girl began to breathe hard and her no's became weaker and less frequent. The danger of being discovered seemed to make it all the more exciting.

It was the first time they'd made love in daylight and they looked at each other before stretching out, full of blushing and pleased shyness. Luis saw the girl's breasts rise and fall with her hard breathing. For some inexplicable reason this was the only woman he desired again immediately after he had her. Silently, wordlessly, with the intimate delight in the passion that had inflamed them like a rocket, they remained wonderfully oblivious of everything, of even themselves, for many minutes. The sun burned their bodies and made the sweat run down their necks.

Finally, Luis sat up. She remained there with her eyes closed, breathing rhythmically. A burning greater than the sun seemed to have enveloped Luis. He leaned over and kissed the curve of her neck.

"I love you very much," he said.

She murmured something happily.

"I love you," he repeated, as though these were the only words he knew.

"And I you," she said from far off. She hadn't opened her eyes.

Luis's fingers, by themselves it seemed, began to become passionate again in their caresses. She pushed him away gently.

"That's enough, Matador."

"Again," he begged, a brown lock of hair down on his damp forehead.

"Calm down — tonight."

He tried to convince her with kisses. He wanted her again, now.

Suddenly something cracked down across his back, right on his old scar. He half straightened up and fell back.

"Maricones de mierda!" Roaring at him from high on his horse was the rancher.

María jumped up, trying to button her shirt. The rancher

raised his quirt again to bring it down on Luis. Camioneto, a few feet behind, shouted.

"Don't hit him, patrón, don't hit him!"

Luis didn't understand what was happening at all, and he sat there on the ground like an idiot with the pain of the whiplash in his back.

"All of you get off my place right now," the rancher rasped to Camioneto. "I don't want any maricones on my hacienda!"

"Let me explain," Camioneto tried to say, "nobody's a maricón here."

"I've got eyes — two men with their arms around each other!"

Camioneto couldn't help laughing. "You didn't see right, patrón. Luis is a man, but the other is a female!"

"What?"

"The one with the light brown hair is a girl."

The rancher didn't say anything for a moment. The earth-colored faces of the two peons behind him didn't change.

"You," said the rancher pointing to María with his quirt, "come here."

She stepped forward up to his horse. The rancher bent down and studied her.

"True what he says?"

"Yes."

The rancher let out a bellowing laugh. "And how come you dress like a man?"

"That's my business."

"And so that's why you two stayed behind." He laughed again.

María lowered her head, turned and mounted her horse silently. Then they all rode off towards the bulls.

39

THE RANCHER UNCORKED THE BOTTLE OF
tequila and filled the two glasses. He pushed one over to the
other man who sat across the pine desk from him.

"Salud."

"Salucita."

They each drank down the liquid at one gulp. The rancher
filled the glasses up again, and took out a cigar.

"Well, then," he said as he lit up, "the business of the boy
is all set?"

The other man shook his head.

"I'd planned on bringing two boys from Mexico City. Two
with names."

"This one's a fine torero, believe me. If he repeats what he
did with my seed bull, he'll blow the top off your bull ring."

The impresario thought a moment. Chucho was an old
friend and an important one. He drank a little of the tequila.

"All right, it's done."

"I've got someone else for your fair too."

"Another torero?" The man frowned, "I can't — "

"A torer*a*."

"Torera?"

"With a pair of ovaries on her."

"Handled them yet, Chucho?"

"Not yet," the manager laughed. "But seriously, she's good.
Take her for the fair."

The impresario looked at him slyly. "You're working her
over, I assume."

Don Chucho smiled vaguely, as though this wouldn't be a bad idea. "A girl bullfighter would be a novelty. Why not try her — not in one of the real novilladas, but in the festival fight."

"What's she look like?"

"Young — "

"Pretty?"

"Very. Want me to call her?"

The boys and María were outside in the sun of the courtyard stripping ears of corn. The rancher came to the door of his office and with one hand at the side of his mouth, he shouted: "María!"

The three turned around. The rancher was motioning at them. Luis frowned.

"Why would they want you?"

She was the most surprised and thought she'd heard wrong. "Why me?"

"How you going to find out," growled Camioneto, "unless you go?"

She ran across the courtyard to the rancher.

"María," he said, putting a big hand on her neck, "there's a man here who wants to speak to you."

They went in.

Luis couldn't take his eyes off the door of the office where the girl had disappeared. He felt a sharp knot in his stomach.

"Bothers you, doesn't it?" said Camioneto.

"Shut up."

"Look, I'm telling you for your own good, Luis, you shouldn't be worrying about this girl one way or another. You should just be thinking about what you're going to do if you get this fight."

"Why don't you lay off?"

"Because I've worked and sweated to help make you a

torero. Because I believe in bullfighting and I believe you're a great bullfighter. But you can't make it mixing women and bulls at this point in your life."

"That same boring sermon."

"I know what I'm talking about. It was a woman that finished me, not a bull. I was through long before that bull crippled me. And this girl will finish you."

"She's not like that."

"She sticks with us now because she's eating. The day she can't use you, she'll give you a kick in the rear and its adiós amigo."

"You're crazy."

After closing the door behind him, Don Chucho gently pushed María into the room.

"Here's your torera."

The impresario poured himself another tequila. She waited for him to say something, but the fat man just looked at her. His eyes were shiny and his face was very red. He belched.

"So you're Don Chucho's torera."

María nodded.

Then he drank and said slyly, "And — do you like to do it?"

María felt herself blush. The same old story. They don't play fair, these birds. Always double-talk, always trying to get you to bed.

"Do what?" she said, innocently.

"Why — fight, of course."

"Ah!"

Don Chucho, his hand still on María, said: "And very well she does it too."

"As I said to Don Chucho, young lady," said the impresario, "I can't pay you anything."

She turned to the rancher and her eyes asked for assistance.

"Hey now," he said, "you can pay her expenses at least."

"Well — " the impresario bit his lips and made as though doing some intricate figuring. "Since it's for Don Chucho, I'll pay your expenses."

"How much?" she asked firmly.

"Let's say fifty pesos."

"That sounds better," said the rancher.

María began to feel on firmer ground. "And how much for the boy?"

"He doesn't interest me," said the man airily, "just you."

Her lips grew thin with fury. She knew for sure now that the last thing that interested him was her talent in the bull ring. She could read in his face the dirty plans he had for her. It was best to lay it on the line straight with pigs like this.

"Either he goes or I don't."

The impresario was taken back for a moment. He looked at Don Chucho who was smiling at the way María had spoken up. The impresario realized he'd have to give in now to ultimately get what he wanted.

"All right. But no money for him."

"That doesn't matter." She'd tell Luis that the fifty was for him and that she was the one who was fighting free.

The rancher held out a glass of tequila. She started to refuse but he insisted. The liquor was strong and made her a little dizzy. Now she felt good with her stomach warmed and her mind just a little hazy. She didn't even pull away when the impresario put his hand on her shoulder.

"Here's to the matadora," he toasted.

The three drank. María put her glass down on the desk. Then with a manly gesture she hooked her thumbs in her pants. "All right, let's have the advance now."

"The what?"

"The advance on the fight."

Don Chucho winked at his friend. "Let's see some money."

"How much," said the man, reluctantly drawing a fat roll from his pants.

"Half," she answered, holding out her hand. He counted out the money, she recounted it, put it in her pocket, and went to the door. She turned and said, "After you see me fight on Sunday it will cost you some more. See you there!"

She left. Chucho went to close the door and watched her run to her friends.

"Spirit, eh?"

"Yes," admitted the impresario. "And she's pretty. But I can handle her." He made a gesture like a matador giving a bull a punishing pass with the muleta. "A couple of trincherazos and I'll bring her into line."

"It's going to be a little harder than that."

"That little tramp? Hah. I bet you I have her in bed by Sunday night."

40

THINGS TURNED OUT WELL, AND LUIS CUT AN ear. María was only fair. While Luis was working over the fourth animal of the afternoon with the muleta, the impresario eased up next to the girl behind the fence.

"Come see me tonight so I can pay you."

"I have to go back to the hacienda," she replied without taking her eyes off Luis.

"Let them go. I'll take you later."

María let out a brief laugh. "That one's pretty old."

"I was thinking of maybe putting you on the card this coming Sunday . . ."

The girl didn't answer but she stepped away from the boards and with her cape on her arm she went over and sat next to Don Chucho further down.

The rancher said as he watched Luis work: "There's a truly great torero inside that boy."

"Yes." Out of the corner of her eye she saw the impresario coming over. Without saying anything he sat next to her, and continued to watch the fight.

"What do you think of Luis Ortega?" asked the rancher.

After a long pause, the impresario said, "I don't like him."

"But just look how the crowd is going for him!"

"I don't care," the man said bitterly, "I don't like his style."

The rancher shrugged his shoulders. Luis was fighting with great feeling, *con hondura* — with deepness. The audience reacted wildly to him, and were now deliriously throwing things down into the ring. The girl hadn't interested them much. Espino, the other boy, had been "discreet" to say the least. Luis Ortega was unquestionably the star of the day. Right now he was lunging at the bull and, with perfect form, was placing the sword right where it should go and right up to the hilt. Now they were giving him the ear, and now, his face bright with joy, he was taking a lap around the ring. This was just a festival, not even in costumes, but if they announced this boy for a real fight, in a suit of lights, for next Sunday, he'd fill the arena as it never had been filled. But the impresario was stubborn.

"I don't like him." He heaved his bulk to his feet and moved away.

Don Chucho turned to María as she watched Luis basking in the applause while he was made to take still another lap around the ring.

"What's between you two?"

"Who?"

"You and the fat one. What'd he say to you?"

She lowered her eyes. "He wanted to see me tonight. I said no."

Luis passed in front of them and jubilantly tossed the ear to María. She leaned forward to catch it. Don Chucho put his hand on her thigh.

"Is he your sweetheart or husband, this Ortega?"

"Does it matter?"

"It could."

"Why?"

"Not only to our friend the impresario. But to me."

"You?"

"You're pretty and you please me. Think it over. If you stay on the hacienda, I could get you a lot of fights. If you need money, you'd just have to ask for it."

She didn't answer. She turned down her mouth and started to move away.

"What do you say?" he called after her.

"I'll think about it," she said.

Luis waved to the crowd for the last time in the center of the ring. Then he sprinted back to the fence and vaulted over it easily. Camioneto gave him a piece of towel to wipe the sweat off his face.

"Where's María?"

"How should I know!" he answered as he began folding the muleta. "Around someplace."

Down the passageway the sour-faced impresario was wad-dling. Luis stopped him.

"It turned out all right, didn't it? I cut an ear."

The man spat and kept walking. "I saw it."

Luis walked along after him. "And wait till you see me in the next fight, I'll cut both ears."

The impresario stopped short. Slowly he took the stub of cigar he was chewing out of his mouth. "Who said you were fighting again?"

Luis began to stammer. "But — I did all right — I cut an ear — "

The man began walking again.

"I'll do better in the next — "

"There's no next one for you."

Desperately, Luis took him by the arm. This was incredible. He had triumphed and the stupidest impresario in the world would realize that he could fill the plaza at twice the prices the following Sunday. He must have misunderstood the man.

"You mean I don't get another fight even after having cut an ear?"

"You don't interest me," said the man, jerking his arm away. "I don't like your style, you're not worth two cents."

Luis stayed there with his mouth open. The wonderful dream had vanished into thin air. He sagged up against the fence and put his head in his hands. But what the devil had happened? Try as he might to keep them back, he felt hot tears of frustration and disappointment in his eyes. Then, as though drunk, he lurched over to where Camioneto was packing up the bundle.

"What's the matter?"

Luis swallowed. "He won't give me the other corrida now."

"After what you did today! The fool!"

Luis pulled himself together. "Where's María?"

She was coming down the passageway, her face serious. She looked at Luis's stricken face and then at Camioneto. She didn't have to ask questions. The three began to walk, crestfallen, silent, oblivious to the friendly words and pats on the back as they made their way through the people back towards the hacienda.

41

THEY CAME BACK INTO TOWN THE NEXT DAY
to pick up their remaining money from the impresario.

"And maybe I can persuade him to put me on this Sunday
after all."

"Look," said Camioneto. "He wouldn't take you as a gift.
The best thing for us to do is get out of here. I heard there's
going to be some fights up in Rodeo this Sunday, if we can
get there in time."

"I still don't get it," said Luis unhappily.

They came to the house at one, as they were told to, and
knocked timidly at the door. An old crone emerged.

"We've come to see the impresario."

"He's eating. Wait."

They crossed the street and sat on a bench.

"I just don't understand it. The crowd was so warm toward me."

"Maybe," said Camioneto, "it's all because someone else
wasn't warm to someone else." He glared at the girl. "Eh,
María?"

"Maybe," she shot back. "But — "

The door opened across the street and the old woman
gestured for them to come. They crossed over and she studied
them with her old eyes for a long moment.

"Which is the girl?"

"Me."

The woman stepped aside. "He wants to see you."

María went in, but as the others tried to follow, the woman said, "Just you," and closed the door in their faces, as Luis protested feebly.

María followed the woman, who was little and wrinkled and smelly, and who shook her head as she walked as though constantly saying no. They walked down a corridor where there were hung cages with twittering birds. In the middle of the patio was a fountain from which a young girl was drawing water.

The old woman stopped in front of a door.

"Knock," she said, and continued down the hall.

María knocked softly. A hoarse voice said to come in.

She found herself in a large room. The sofa and chairs were of rattan. In one corner, near the window that opened onto the street, was a big antique desk. María saw the impresario as he swiveled around in his chair to face her.

"Come close." He pointed to a chair. "Sit down."

The girl took off her cap and remained standing. The fat man leaned back to study her better. Smiling, he tugged at his lower lip. His eyes were almost lost in the puffiness around them.

"You are very good, a very good torera."

"Thank you." María lowered her head.

He motioned with his hand. "Come closer."

She took a step.

"Closer so that we can converse like decent folk, without having to almost shout at each other."

She took another step.

"You're very lovely, child."

"Thank you."

"And brave. Why do you bullfight?"

"Because I like it."

"What — what else do you like to do?"

"Nothing."

"Nothing?"

"Nothing."

"You like this boy, don't you?"

"Perhaps."

He got up and came closer. She saw he had egg stains on his shirt. He came next to her and stroked her cheek gently. "Would you like to fight this Sunday?"

"And the boy?"

"Let him scratch for himself. I'm not interested in him."

"I'm not interested in you, either."

The man smiled a little. He reached out his hand and opened a tin box on his desk. He held his face next to hers. "See that? Two hundred pesos."

"I just came for the twenty-five you owe us."

"These two hundred are for you."

" 'Course, they're a present," said María, with a wry smile.

"They're for you if you fight on Sunday, and if you're — friendly."

"I just want what's coming to me."

He started towards her, his eyes shining, breathing hard. She backed up, never taking her eyes off his face as one would do with a bull. Mentally, she was locating the door behind her. She trusted her agility to get her out of this one. Every muscle in her lithe body was tense and ready. The fat man saw what she was up to and started to head her off. María turned and sprang for the door, but the man, with surprising speed, got there first and blocked her way.

Until now, María hadn't really been frightened. In the time she'd been in the "wars," she'd been in similar situations several times. Then she'd never really been afraid, perhaps because she believed that being a virgin, nothing could happen to her. Now that she wasn't, she was terrified, convinced that if this creature once got his hands on her . . .

"Don't be a fool," he was mouthing. "I'll give you whatever you want, all the money . . ."

María had put four yards between him and herself. She knew there was no escape by the door. He hadn't moved, knowing there was no escape for her. He'd stay there all the time necessary to convince her. He looked calm, though his abdomen heaved with his breathing.

"One way or another, I'm going to have you, so let's make it the decent way, eh?"

María had worked around in front of the window. It had no grill and it opened onto the street. The important thing was the knob, to get it turned without his knowing.

"And if I don't want to, then what?"

With his sleeve the man wiped the sweat from his forehead. "In Nombre de Dios, I'm the boss. All I do is order the police and they put the three of you in jail. Very easy."

"That's what you say" — her hands were behind her back now and her fingers found the knob. Slowly she turned it.

"I say it and I mean it, child," said the big man, calmly. "In half an hour I'll have you all in — "

She turned the knob all the way and banged open the paned doors. Whirling, she leaped out, one hand on the sill as though vaulting the barrera. She fell sprawling on the street, but got quickly to her feet and started sprinting.

The two boys saw her running desperately, and heard her shout: "Run for it!"

They sprang up and ran after her with all the speed in their legs.

"Here we go again," said Luis, thinking of his escape from Fresnillo.

The fat impresario made it to the window in time to see

them round the corner and then he began to holler at the top
of his lungs: "Grab them, they've robbed me!"

42

"YOU'RE TOO LATE." IT WAS THE IMPRESARIO
of the Rodeo arena speaking, a bilious, pompous little man
who also acted as presidente municipal for the city.

"Look, Señor Presidente, Ortega cut an ear last Sunday,
and they carried him out of the plaza on their shoulders."

"Where was that?"

"In Villa de Nombre de Dios."

"And the girl, is she any good?"

"Terrific," said Camioneto. "A second Conchita Cintrón."

"Look, I don't have anything for the boy, but the girl I can
use."

Damn her, he thought. "Well, better than nothing."

"I've got one extra bull, and since they've never seen a
woman fighting in these parts, we could give it a try."

"And about the parné — what about that?"

"About what?"

"The money."

"Uy! Look, the others doing the cowboy stuff tomorrow
are all ranchers and they're doing it for free. Any money we
take is for repairing the church."

"You pay the boardinghouse," Camioneto proposed, "and
the expenses, we'll say, are twenty pesos."

"Let's split it — call it ten."

He held out his hand to close the deal. Camioneto shook it.
"Done."

They were put in one room. The boardinghouse keeper didn't know anything about bullfighting, but she knew how to take care of hungry people at the dinner table. In the room there was only one double bed. The three of them looked at it. María put her things on it. Camioneto sprang over beside her, grabbed the girl's bundle, and tossed it on the ground.

Luis planted himself in front of him, furious. Camioneto calmly lay down on the ancient rose-colored mattress.

"Tonight I'm sleeping in a bed even if the Pope tries to stop me."

"She's a woman," Luis said. "Let her have the bed."

"Why should I? Just cause she's female? What do I care?" He winked suggestively. "Now if she wants to sleep in bed let her — and you sleep on the floor."

Luis grabbed Camioneto by his shirt and shook him.

"Let him go, Luis," said María. "We'll work it out."

And that night, for the first time in a long time, Camioneto slept comfortably in a bed. Luis and María chose to stay together on the floor, wrapped up in the capes.

For the last act on the program, on this hot, sticky Sunday afternoon, they turned loose a young bull for the señorita torera, María Valente. The bull, although not too big or strong, was difficult. In the first part of the fight she could do little but try to stay a good distance away on the passe and defend herself as best she could. The spectators began to shout, demanding that she place her own banderillas. Luis was starting out with a pair of the sticks when she called to him.

"Bring them here!"

Luis was astonished.

"But you don't know how — "

The crowd was yelling harder and getting nastier. María grabbed the sticks and headed out for the bull, saying to Luis, "Be quiet — "

Quickly Luis turned to get his cape to help her. Camioneto, who had heard the brief exchange, grabbed him.

"Leave her alone. Don't meddle, or the hicks will come down on top of you."

With her arms raised high, her body arched gracefully, María went out towards the animal. Luis didn't take his eyes off her for a second, his cape ready in his hands and his body tense to run to her aid.

"She's got a good ass on her," Camioneto commented.

Luis didn't even dare to turn away for an instant to glare at him. The bull kept pawing the sand, without making up its mind to charge. It was a little animal, two years old and weighing about five hundred pounds. María kept coming, step by step, closer and closer to it. "She's not leaving herself any exit," Camioneto foresaw, and his heart leapt with pleasure. The girl was getting herself into an impossible terrain. Around her echoed the shouts, the howls of the audience. Actually, she knew nothing about the science of placing banderillas, but she sensed that she had walked up too close to the horns. That black and hairy creature now bellowed once and lunged forward suddenly, making the ground under the girl's feet shudder with its weight. She closed her eyes, stuck out her arms, and waited for something to happen.

The moment the animal charged, Luis knew it was going to catch her. Rapidly, he ran out towards the center where the animal and the girl were coming together. The bull crashed against the girl with surprising violence and hurled her body into the air. When she fell, María was at its mercy. The beast went for her, hooking her, stepping on her, lifting her off the ground and slamming her to the sand.

"Ea, toro! Ea, toro!" Luis shouted frantically, trying to lure it off her by flashing the cape in its face.

Camioneto suddenly was there and darting in, with no cape, he somehow grabbed María and dragged her out from under the animal's feet. The crowd laughed and howled with pleasure. Luis stayed out in the center with the bull, keeping it from attacking again, as Camioneto carried her off.

Camioneto laid María down behind the fence. The girl's eyes were closed and her face covered with blood. Futilely, they tried to bring her to.

"Goddamn!" Camioneto muttered, afraid now.

Luis came running up and knelt beside the girl.

"Look — "

From her waist down María was covered with blood. It was streaming down her leg frighteningly.

Stunned, Luis breathed: "A terrible one," and he thought instantly of Juanito Lavín.

Camioneto started to examine the wound, but Luis grabbed his arm.

"Leave her alone. Lift her feet up."

Between them they lifted her. There was a great blotch of blood left on the sand, the same blood that kept dripping as they went, marking their course in red. Now around the ring was a strange silence. Many of the ranchers took off their sombreros, in a gesture of respect. Several crossed themselves as though she were already dead. But the program had to go on. When Camioneto and Luis, followed by some curious children, came out into the street, the crowd was already laughing at the drunken antics of two brave fellows who were trying to fight the bull by holding a serape between them.

The blood didn't stop flowing. Not in drops now, but flooding from the girl in a steady gush.

"A terrible one, a terrible one," Luis kept gasping. He didn't care whether or not Camioneto saw the tears streaming down his cheeks.

They put María on the bed. She was breathing, but her eyes were shut. The boardinghouse keeper fluttered in, and she and Luis started to undress her.

"Camioneto," Luis ordered. "Go find a doctor!"

"Where?"

"Doctor Rosas lives a block up," said the woman. "Tell him that Doña Jovita wants him."

Five minutes later Camioneto was back with the doctor. María still hadn't moved. The doctor was a young man with a sad square face. He said hello briefly and then knelt beside the bed. He put his ear to the girl's breast. When he got up he took off his jacket. Then he opened up the bag he'd brought.

"What happened?" he said to the boys. "The girl's in a bad way."

"We're the toreros, doctor. In the ring — she was placing banderillas when — "

"All right, all right," the doctor cut them off as he rolled up his sleeves.

He lifted off the blanket that covered the girl's body. Luis and Camioneto were shocked to see the enormous red splotch María was lying in. The doctor jerked his head at them.

"Please leave."

Luis stayed there, staring, hypnotized by the quantity of blood. She must have been all broken inside. Camioneto tugged at him.

"Come outside."

A long half hour went by. They smoked ceaselessly and silently. Down deep, Camioneto was glad. He hated women that tried to invade an art that belonged to men exclusively, and nothing was too bad for them. But he hated to see Luis like this.

Luis was shattered. His tears hadn't stopped for a moment, wetting his hands and his cigarette. "I shouldn't have let her, I shouldn't have let her." He kept staring at the door which remained closed. He started to get up and go to her. Camioneto stopped him.

"Take it easy. Maybe it's nothing too serious."

"She's got a bad one, a bad one," he kept repeating.

Doña Jovita came out fast, banging the door closed. She didn't stop to answer when Luis asked what was happening. They heard her heels clicking down the stairs. In a moment she was back with a folded sheet under her arm and a kettle of hot water in her hands.

"My goodness, my goodness," she said over and over.

Another fifteen minutes went by. Camioneto suddenly asked: "Why don't you leave her once and for all?"

"Leave her?"

"That's what I said. Drop her, before she drops you."

"You starting on that again?" Luis was too destroyed to get angry. "She's like this and you're starting on that again?"

The door finally opened. The doctor appeared, fixing his cuff links. Luis ran to him and grabbed him by the arms.

"What's the matter with her, doctor? Is it bad?"

The doctor shook his head.

"It's not bad, luckily. The fetus was expelled."

"The what? And the wound?"

"She just aborted. Got rid of a two-months-old fetus, that's all."

Luis pulled away and ran into the room. Camioneto took care of the doctor's fee. Doña Jovita started collecting the bloody sheets. María was very pale and sweaty, with her short hair moist on her temples. On the pillow was a spot of saliva.

"María," Luis moaned, kneeling by her.

Doña Jovita left the room. María turned her head on the pillow. Her half-closed eyes looked at Luis. She tried a smile.

"Doctor tell you?" she said with difficulty.

"Yes. I thought it was a horn wound."

There was a pause. María made a great effort to talk. Her

jaws were as heavy as lead. Her whole body ached.

"I had a child of yours in my stomach."

Luis had started crying again. He didn't know whether with sadness or happiness.

"If I'd kept on going with him inside, I wouldn't have been able to bullfight."

"Of course." Sliding his fingers under the sheet, he stroked one of María's hot hands.

"I —" the girl took a breath, "I didn't know I was sick."

"It doesn't matter."

She tried to smile. "Can you imagine a pregnant bull-fighter?"

Doña Jovita had closed the shutters and the room was almost dark. It was warm and it smelled strange. María perspired copiously. Luis stroked her forehead.

"I don't want that to happen again," she said.

Luis agreed. It would never happen again, that was for sure. He couldn't quite believe he'd actually created a child. The first of his life. He liked the fact that it was with María, even though it had been lost. He didn't know how to keep from having it happen again, but he'd ask Camioneto.

"There must be a way so it doesn't happen again," he reassured her.

"I like you very much, Luis."

"I like you too."

"The doctor says I better stay in bed a few days."

"Many as you want."

"I don't want it. He says rest if I don't want to injure myself inside."

"That's fine."

"Because if I injure myself, I can't ever get pregnant again . . ."

43

THAT NIGHT WHEN LUIS ASKED CAMIONETO
how to avoid getting María pregnant again, he answered:
"Very simple. Leave her."

They were sitting on the leather-covered chairs in the hall
outside the room where the girl slept.

"Don't you see how she messes up your life? This time it
turned out all right. But what about the next time?"

Camioneto could be right. María was starting to be a com-
plication. She was a woman and women were always coming
down with strange things. A wife was just bad business for
a torero and that's what María was becoming, more or less.
A married matador is a finished matador, everyone said. And
how was she helping him? When he was out with the bulls he
couldn't really concentrate for wondering who might be flirt-
ing with her or propositioning her in the passageway. And
when she was out there fighting he died a thousand deaths for
fear of what could happen to her.

But lord, how he loved to be with her, especially at night.
And since he'd been the first, he felt very possessive about
her. She was his property exclusively and the thought of her
ever belonging to someone else was highly painful.

"So you better leave her, and soon," Camioneto was saying.

"But what would she do? She needs us."

"She got along fine before we met her."

"It's different now."

"Because she's your mistress."

"Maybe."

"She's a tramp, Luis. She wants to get someplace in this world at the cost of anyone and anything."

"Don't say that."

"Well, it's true."

"She's good. Maybe we should separate, but she's good."

"You'll find out one of these days. The real ambition and the real badness hasn't come out yet."

Luis stretched out in his chair and tried to make himself go to sleep. He stared up at the ceiling in the gloom for a long time. Then he said resolutely: "As soon as she gets well, I'm going to straighten things out."

44

SIX DAYS LATER, WITH FIVE PESOS IN THE community kitty, they arrived at Parral. It was fair time and there was gaiety in the air. On the street corners were posters telling of this Sunday's "festival" fight. It turned out that the impresario was Blind Muñoz, an old friend of Camioneto's, and he found him in the Café Palacio. He told him about Luis and the girl.

"So you've got a torera on the string, eh?" said Blind Muñoz, scratching his cadaverous face and blinking his myopic eyes. "Is she pretty? Maybe I could use her."

"Sure. But what about Luis?"

"I told you, not a chance. Unless — " he scrubbed his chin — "perhaps I could put him on in the clown part, the charlot stuff."

"Luis — as a charlot? With a calf? This boy is a great torero!"

"We're all great in the cafés."

Camioneto shook his head. "Well, I guess it's better than nothing. I'll go tell them."

They rented a room in a boardinghouse. Luis and María had the bed and Camioneto slept on the capes on the floor. The café transaction hadn't pleased Luis, but he said nothing. María, on the other hand, was happy and talked of nothing else after seeing the animals, of what she would do with the one she would draw. Luis brooded in silence. He felt humiliated at having agreed to do something he abhorred. There was nothing comic about bullfighting to him, and therefore, comic bullfighting had no place in the spectacle. Without knowing why, he blamed the girl for this and felt a hatred for her deep inside him. It was best to end this once and for all.

He lay awake long after the others were asleep. One moment he promised himself to break it off definitely in the morning, and in the next, he was admitting to himself that he loved her too much to leave her. He knew deep inside that he would never leave her, that she would have to be the one to leave him.

He was still awake at dawn. "Me a charlot — " he gritted his teeth and turned his face to the wall.

The little arena was full when, at four o'clock in the afternoon, they made the parade into the ring. The boy from Chihuahua and Jesús Muñoz were dressed in real "suits of lights," María in the bolero jacket of the *corto* costume, and Luis in the *pachuco* clown outfit.

María pleased the crowd with her farol passes, her gaoneras, and her chicuelinas. But she pleased them even more with the way she moved her hips when she walked. From the passageway, Luis watched with jealousy and shame. "She's a tramp," he said between his teeth.

Before the final phase, Blind Muñoz advised her, "Dedicate to that man up there" — he pointed to a youngish man in the first row — "he has money."

With the sword and muleta clamped in her left hand, she took off her hat with her right and dedicated the death of the bull to the man. Then, walking provocatively across the ring amidst lurid cat calls from the audience, she began to pass the animal with the muleta. She did so well that when she killed with one thrust, they gave her an ear.

When she went back for her hat, the man to whom she'd dedicated said, "You're a fine torera. There's a little present for you" — he pointed inside the hat — "in here."

He threw it down to her and she found a fifty-peso bill inside. Carefully she folded it, put it in her pocket and went back to looking at the fight.

If the crowd was kind to María, they were quite the opposite to Luis. As a comic bullfighter, he was a total flop, and the two or three good passes he made with the muleta weren't taken seriously because of the smallness of the animal. Then, determined not to be outdone by the girl, Luis suddenly knelt down with his back to the bull. It decided to charge at that moment, knocked him to the sand, and then roughed him up on the ground. They carried him unconscious to the fence. While Camioneto splashed water in his face to revive him, the crowd began to chant for María to substitute for the clown.

"Get out there!" said Blind Muñoz, handing her Luis's muleta.

Back in the hotel, Luis decided to lie down for a while. His body and arms ached terribly and his face was swollen where the animal had stepped on him. María was putting on her make-up in front of the little mirror on the dresser. Without turning around she asked: "How did I look today, Luis?"

He muttered: "You moved your buttocks fine."

She turned smiling, a tube of lipstick in her hands. "Really?"

"Too damned much."

"But the crowd loved it, didn't they? So it doesn't matter." She turned back. "You just sort of lost your head and went to pieces didn't you."

"I know," he muttered. "I know."

"The trouble is you don't really know how to run your hand, you keep your elbow too close to your body."

"You don't say!"

"That's why you have a hard time."

Luis hated her very much then. He wanted to be alone with his terrible flop and his pain. He didn't want to be told any more painful things today. What did she care? She had been great, and triumph sparkled in her breast like sweet drunkeness.

She leaned against the foot of the bed.

"Shall we eat?"

"I'm not hungry."

"But I am."

"Have some food brought here, why don't you?"

"I want to go out."

"I tell you I don't feel like it."

"All right, I'll go alone."

Luis felt a jealous fear in his stomach. He couldn't let her go out alone even if he were dying. Camioneto came in at that moment.

"What's up?" he asked, sensing the tension.

Luis feigned sleepiness. "Take her out for something to eat, will you?"

"And you?"

"I'll grab some sleep. You go with her . . ."

45

ON THE WAY TO THE CAFE MARIA SAID: "STILL
can't stand me, can you."

"That's right."

"Why?"

"Because you're poison."

"Jealous?"

"Call it whatever you damn well feel like."

A car passed and they had to stop for a moment. There
were throngs of gay people in the street and a heavy luke-
warmness in the dusty air. They started walking again.

"You think that Luis will ever be a matador?"

"And one of the greats of all time."

"There's something —" she frowned, "something about
him I don't like."

"As a man or as a torero?"

"Torero naturally," she shot back. "He doesn't really have
much confidence, no real decision. He won't get anyplace
that way."

"What do you think I've been telling him? If he once
makes up his mind — if he just gets his life unmessed up —
and really makes up his mind — then you'll see the greatest
torero in Mexico since Gaona."

"And I suppose I'm the mess."

"All right — yes."

"I help him — not hurt him. If it hadn't been for me he
wouldn't have fought in Nombre de Dios or Rodeo or here."

"You're just a novelty."

"You're damn right I am." She put her hands on her hips. "So you two better be nice to me."

Without stopping, Camioneto took her by the elbow. He saw the mocking smile on the girl's lips. She was so sure of herself now. Clearly she thought she was the shining light of the bull world. Her gesture, her tone — obviously one of those who couldn't take success, even a little success.

"You're right," said Camioneto. "Luis and I are a couple of pimps for you, just bums. So why don't you go your own way?"

She kept smiling. "Supposing I want to stay with Luis."

"You going to tell me you love him?"

"He pleases me. And I intend to stay."

In the café the toreros were celebrating. They had pushed several tables together to make one large one and they were all crowded around it. They were talking over the day's fight. When Chucho Muñoz saw them come in, he stood up and applauded María.

They hastened to make room for her, congratulating her on the performance as they did. María found herself sitting next to a familiar looking man who was holding out a rum drink to her. Then Muñoz, raising his orange drink, proposed a toast.

"For María Valente, queen of the bulls!"

"Hear, hear," the others chorused.

The man next to María rested his chin on the girl's shoulder and breathed alcoholically in her face. She pulled away.

"Don't you know me?"

María had been trying to place his face. It was a pleasant face, of about thirty, which frequently laughed loudly. His hands were large and his elegant suit was of gray cashmere.

"To tell the truth . . ." María began.

He put his arm around the back of her chair and his fingers caressed her off shoulder.

"Forgotten me so soon? Even though I gave you fifty pesos?"

"Oh! You're the one."

"The same. And here I thought you dedicated the bull to me because you liked my looks."

"I'm afraid it was because someone told me you weren't too hard to get money out of."

He laughed and gave her arm a suggestive squeeze. "And I'm not."

She sipped her rum drink. He looked at her, the smile never leaving his lips. He liked the girl. He thought: "Dressed as a woman and up close she's really very lovely."

María felt a pair of eyes, cold and hard as chisels, digging into her. She turned to face Camioneto. His face was brown and angry. She turned away with a shrug. To hell with him. Her companion was saying to her under his breath: "When something pleases me, I pay. No matter how much."

"You must be very rich."

"My father's a millionaire, so I have a bit."

"It must be nice to be able to say that."

"Nicer to be able to get what you want."

"Like?"

"Look — " He put his hand in his pants and pulled out a roll of bills. It looked like a fortune to María. "Look: with this I can buy anything."

"Maybe so."

María finished her drink. He filled it up again. She felt a little dizzy but not hungry, even though she hadn't eaten for fifteen hours.

"What do you say?" he suddenly said.

"To what?"

"A walk?"

"And what do I get out of it?"

"You'll see."

"Thanks, but I didn't come alone." She indicated Camioneto with her head.

Manuel Salgado, as he'd said his name was, shrugged.

"If he's your husband, leave him."

"If I went with you," she said without blinking, "it wouldn't be just for a few moments."

"So?"

"We might fall in love," lied María. "And then I'd have to stay here."

Salgado shook his head. "Bit naïve, this business of falling in love. I'm married. All I want is for you to be nice to me — and I'll be good to you."

"I've heard that before, and nothing good has ever come of it."

"They didn't know how to treat you the way you deserve. You have to talk real money to beautiful women. I liked you so I gave you fifty pesos. It could be a lot more. What do you say?"

"It's worth thinking about."

Manuel Salgado put his hand in his pocket again and from the roll he peeled two bills. He held them in one hand and nudged her. She shook her head. He added a fifty-peso bill. She shook her head again. He added still another bill.

"Take it," he said, pushing the bills into her hand.

The money burned as it lay there in her unclosed palm. It was the first time she'd taken money from a man this way. For a moment she was going to give them back to Salgado, to shout in his face that she was no whore that he could just buy. But it was only a moment. Her heart was beating hard and she felt that her face was the color of a muleta. Confused, she lowered her eyes and stayed like that for several minutes. And Luis? He loved her, protected her, was jealous of her. What Salgado was proposing, what he was paying for, no woman could listen to without being insulted. It was buying her for a while. Renting her for half an hour.

And Luis? The name kept hammering at her brain. But after all, even though they were lovers, nothing really bound her to him. You don't love him, she told herself. You sleep in his bed but you don't really feel part of him, the way they say one feels when really in love. He's just your friend, your peón. He can't give you anything. On the contrary, it's you who do the giving. But this man here gives you money. Good money, in exchange for nothing, practically nothing. If you do what he wants, Luis would never know. It's a chance to pick up a few pesos. In this life money comes first. With money there's nothing you can't do.

That was it. What did Luis matter? Or Camioneto? Or even herself? What mattered was money, those little bills that made dreams come true. Salgado wanted her tonight and he'd pay to have her. It would just be a question of a moment, to do something that wasn't really very hard to do. Why hadn't she thought of this before? She opened her hand and looked at the bills on her palm for an instant. She raised her eyes.

"Well," she said, "what are we waiting for?"

They left without saying goodbye to anyone. Camioneto started to follow, but Chucho Muñoz put his heavy gnarled hand on his shoulder. When Salgado and María had left the café, Pancho spat out: "Lousy buñí!"

"Let her do what she wants," Muñoz advised.

"I don't care for her sake — just Luis's."

"If she's his, let him watch out for her."

"She's a tramp."

"Name me one that isn't." Muñoz smiled. "Getting back to what I was saying, you could go from here up to Camargo where I understand there's going to be a real . . ."

Camioneto wasn't listening.

Luis was awake. When Camioneto came in the room he found him leafing through an old copy of the magazine *Esto*.

"And María?"

With his back to Luis, Camioneto unfolded the capes on which he slept. "I don't know."

"What do you mean you don't know?"

"She left the café a while ago. I thought she'd be here."

Luis jumped up from the bed and shook him. Camioneto was ashamed to look him in the face. He knew he hadn't acted as a good friend, that in a way he'd been an accomplice to the treachery. Luis was pale now with jealousy. His lips trembled as he said: "How long ago did she leave?"

"Half an hour," said Camioneto, though it was closer to two hours.

"Alone?"

"Of course."

Luis shook him again.

"Why didn't you come with her?"

With a jerk Camioneto freed himself from Luis's grasp. He pushed Luis away and with his jaw jutting out he exploded.

"I'm sick of these messes because of this woman! If she's yours, then watch her yourself. If you're going to sleep with her, you better stick to her petticoats so others don't get the same idea!"

Luis let his arms drop to his sides. Slowly he backed up to the bed and let himself drop there heavily. Camioneto watched him cry with silent fury. He knew his friend was suffering the most violent pangs of jealousy, and he felt a little sorry for him. Not very, though, because he believed a little suffering made character, and Luis could use a bit of that. He wrapped himself up in the capes, rested his head on a muleta and closed his eyes for sleep.

An hour went by before he heard Luis moving about in the

room. A little later there came the noise of a woman's laughter, and the hoarse echo of a man's. Then the squeal of a car starting off. In a moment the door squeaked open. Luis snapped on the light. Camioneto opened his eyes and saw María coming in on tiptoes.

"Where the hell have you been?" Luis bellowed as he threw himself at her.

Surprised, she stammered: "In the café — I've just come from there and . . ."

"Lying bitch!"

The crack of his hand echoed in the room as he hit her. María began to cry. Luis threw her on the bed and then stood over her.

Let them work it out between themselves, Camioneto said to himself, and the pleasant thought came that now María would surely leave the torero.

"Who were you with? Where'd you go, you lousy whore?"

She half sat up. Her hair was over her tear-flooded eyes. With his threatening fists Luis looked prepared to kill her. He raised his arm. Instinctively she threw herself on him to protect herself. They struggled. From his corner Camioneto could see the battle of the shadows on the ceiling. Suddenly the cries of the girl and Luis's insults ceased. There was silence.

Then the light was put out, and the bed began creaking under the weight of their bodies.

"Stupid brute!" Camioneto hissed, covering his head with the cape.

46

"THE IMPRESARIO AT JUAREZ BETTER HAVE lots of money to pay me," said Luis, tipping up the bottle of tequila.

"Look, Luis," said Camioneto, "we've got a good break here, maybe the best chance you've had. Don't get big ideas."

"You'll see how I do."

"We never would have got the fight if I hadn't caught the impresario's cousin when he was drunk. You got to be good."

"Don't worry."

María listened, bored. The platform car swayed from side to side as the freight rattled along through the cold night. Behind them the chains creaked that held the six shipping crates containing the bulls. The overseer and two vaqueros drowsed up against the crates on the leeward side. One of them sleepily lit a cigar.

"Give me a drink for the cold," said the girl.

Luis passed over the bottle. She took a big drink and offered it to Camioneto, who refused it. Luis took it back and tipped it up.

"You been drinking too much the last weeks." Camioneto pointed to the unseen bulls that occasionally shifted their weight restlessly and snorted in their crates. "They weigh one hell of a lot, Luis."

"Christ, I'm just supposed to fight them," Luis retorted, "not lift them!"

The girl laughed, and Luis laughed too. He started to drink again.

"I'm telling you cut it out," said Camioneto.

"Why?"

"Because when you flop I flop."

"What does it matter if he has a little fun?" said the girl. "Can't train all the time."

Luis stood up and signaled María to follow him. Walking unsteadily, trying to counteract the tequila as well as the motion of the train, they headed for the opposite end of the platform car. Between two of the crates there was an open, protected space.

"Lie down," Luis mumbled.

The girl stretched out next to him.

At noon the freight train pulled into the station at Ciudad Juárez. It was hot, and suspended in the blue sky was a huge cream-colored cloud. The platform car was uncoupled from the train and shunted off to a siding. Two big trucks backed up to the flatcar. When they had the trucks up against it, the boys saw a tall man in a dark suit emerge from the cab of one of the vehicles.

"Which of you is Luis Ortega?"

"Me," Luis said, jumping down.

"My cousin called me this morning."

Camioneto and María came up and Luis introduced them to the impresario of the bull ring of the city of Ciudad Juárez.

"Who's this one?" he asked, looking at the girl.

"She fights too."

"I mean is she your wife — mistress?"

"She just goes along with us."

"That's good. I don't like pimps."

"Sí, señor," said Luis, taken aback a bit.

"I got you a room in the hotel. But just one. I didn't know you weren't alone."

"We'll arrange it." And then Luis said: "Oiga, patrón — who am I on the program with?"

"With Fernando López — and Rafaelillo."

47

CAMIONETO PUSHED OPEN THE DOOR AND WAS surprised to find the blinds drawn. María and Luis were still sleeping, and it was past one o'clock in the afternoon. Camioneto opened a window. Outside the temperature was sweltering and the white fronts of the houses glistened in the heat. His foot struck an empty bottle of tequila.

"Get up, you bum!"

"Little more sleep," was the mumbled answer.

"Christ, it's late!"

"Beat it and leave us alone."

Camioneto was in no mood for this. He had the time carefully allotted for getting Luis dressed and seeing that all the things were arranged. He grabbed the bedclothes and stripped them off. The fact that both María and Luis were naked didn't bother him. The girl, furious, struggled to cover herself. Luis swung on Camioneto but missed. His head swam and there was an ache behind his eyes.

"You're still drunk," Camioneto roared.

Luis didn't answer and sitting on the edge of the bed he hid his face in his hands. He let some bitter spit drool down on the floor between his feet. María got up, wrapped in a sheet, and went to the bathroom. "All week — ever since we've been here — you've been drinking tequila on top of that woman!"

"For the love of God dry up!"

"You'll see once you get out in that ring."

"What time is it?"

"Almost two."

"Did you go to the drawing?"

"Think I was going to wait for you to get up? You drew the two biggest."

Luis reacted, his chin wavering slightly. "The biggest? They must have pulled a fast one on you."

"What does it matter?" Camioneto's face twisted in a leer. "Weren't you the one who said he could handle anything?"

Nobody could have tricked Pancho Camioneto into drawing the two worst bulls. But when they were pairing off the animals with the representatives of the other novilleros, he had deliberately, and to the surprise of the others, asked for the two biggest and toughest looking ones of the six. His conscience didn't bother him at all; he prayed that they'd turn out as rough as possible and teach Luis Ortega the lesson he so badly needed.

"Get in there and get a cold shower!"

"I'll be all right," Luis mumbled. "I'm a little dizzy right now, but I'll be fine once I get in the ring."

When they turned the sixth bull of the afternoon out of the toril tunnel, Luis resolved to do well or end up in the infirmary. Things had turned out badly on his first bull. It wasn't a question of luck. The bull was bad, it was true. But other times he'd had bad bulls and had the guts and decision to correct their dangerous faults and get a decent performance out of them. But today he couldn't keep his feet from jumping all over the place. The crowd came down on top of him, hurling insults and even cushions at him. As he came over to the fence Camioneto called him a fairy son of a whore.

"I'll do better on my next one," Luis had muttered.

Now his second bull was in the ring. The banderillero, Tabaquito, went out and tried it out so that Luis could see how it charged. It charged hard, but honestly and cleanly with no tricks. As he set it up for him along the fence, the banderillero shouted: "Let's go now — here's a great one, one to make history with!"

Of course he was going to make history with this animal! Luis got the cape right in his hands. He went out in the ring with his body erect and challenged the bull.

"Ah hah toro! Ah hah, bonito!"

Then it charged.

Leaning up against the fence Rafaelillo smoked casually. His cynical black eyes kept watching the marionette which was dancing so unattractively out there in front of the bull.

Luis had tried to stand up to the bull but he hadn't been able to, and when the bull's instinct realized the man was afraid, it took over the ring.

The crowd booed. Camioneto yelled: "Hold your ground — don't move those feet!" But Luis was deaf and blind, broken inside. His arms were dead arms, his legs were mutinous and wobbly with fear. Everything was going around. He looked up at the huge crowd and in his impotence he wanted to throw himself on their mercy; but in front of him he saw no human faces, only a cruel, multi-colored blur.

"Stand still, you son of a bitch," Camioneto was yelling. "Stand still!"

And that was precisely what he would have liked to do, what he was trying desperately to do. But he could not. His fear was greater than his will.

People began to leave. Rafaelillo moved down the passage-way and leaned up against the fence next to María.

"You know something?" he said with a smile. "Your man's a bum."

"I know," she answered, without looking away from Luis as he tried to control the animal with the muleta cape.

"How long you been with him?"

"About four months."

"I have to admire your guts."

"Why do you say that?"

"To stick with that oaf."

"I know what I'm doing."

"I've known him for a long time. He claimed he was a good torero."

"And he is! Anyone can have an off day."

"Ortega is a bum who is never going anyplace in bullfight-ing."

"What do you know about it?"

"All I have to do is look. Take me: I fight every Sunday, make good money. And him, he's going to die of hunger." He turned and looked at her. "You're beautiful, you know."

"Yes?"

"What you and I could do!"

"Like what?"

"We'd go great! We'd make a team, fight on the same program. We'd have more contracts than we could handle."

"Sounds fine, but maybe you're a bum too."

Rafaelillo's sensuous lips widened in a smile and his dark eyes flashed with a brilliance that could be caused by either hate or pleasure. María looked back at him without blinking. He really was good-looking. His suit was elegant and he smelled clean and good. There was something very attractive about him, an attractive lawlessness, that appealed to her. Besides, he was the first famous torero she had met. She ran her fingers over the epaulets of his costume. The roughness of the goldwork gave her a tingling feeling.

"Pretty uniform, eh? Cost me three thousand. Next Sunday I'm trying out a new one."

"Where you fighting?"

"Laredo. Why — " he looked at her deeply — "Why don't you come with me?"

She shook her head.

He pursued it. "You wouldn't be sorry. I've got money and I'd like to spend it on you."

María shook her shoulders, dusted off her clothes, and moved away. Rafaelillo tossed away his cigarette and watched her pensively, confidently, as she went over to Camioneto.

"Well," Camioneto spat out, "there's the fairy you've made out there!"

María grabbed him by the shoulder.

"It's my fault that he's got no balls?"

"He's got all the balls in the world!" Camioneto spat back, "or rather he did before he met you!"

"When I stink out there in the ring I don't try to blame it on someone else!"

"He's not blaming you, I am!"

"Tell him to get rid of me then!"

"He's an idiot with no will power. If you were mine I would have given you a kick in the ass long ago!"

"I don't think this is going on much longer anyway," she said. She watched Luis coming over to the fence to exchange the wooden sword for the real one, tears streaming down his cheeks.

48

LUIS WAS LYING DOWN ON THE BED SMOKING when María came back to the room. Camioneto had gone to the drugstore for some medicine for Luis. The girl felt good, and a little tight. Through the window came the pale rays of the street lights and the neon signs.

"Where you been?"

From inside her dress as she stripped it over her head, María answered: "I took a walk around the park. It was hot here."

She was lying. The last two hours she had spent upstairs in Rafaelillo's room with him and his friends. She had had half a dozen drinks and had begun to feel warm and sexy. Rafaelillo was a pleasant, generous, extremely attractive man who sang flamenco songs and told off-color stories amusingly. As she watched him María felt a great attraction for him and she wanted him to ask her to sleep with him after the others had gone. But Rafaelillo limited himself to telling her repeatedly that she was beautiful and that she should go away with him. He told her again of the many advantages he could offer her. All she had to do was say yes.

And María did say yes, that it sounded good to her. Rafaelillo, in a happy mood, shook hands with her elaborately, jokingly, and congratulated her on her intelligence. Then he said, indicating the pretty blonde across the room talking to one of his friends, "I brought that gachí with me and before you and I can get together I have to unload her."

"And when will that be?"

"Tomorrow or the day after, at the most. In any event I'll expect you Sunday in Laredo, right?"

"Right," said María. And she let the torero's hand prowl around her upper leg.

She wasn't jealous because her new friend would be spending a few more days with the girl who had come from Mexico with him. María could wait as long as necessary. Actually, the idea of leaving Luis hadn't just come on her. Luis pleased her in bed. But out of it he had turned into a cowardly bum who let himself be pushed around by his manager. If Camioneto hadn't come between them, the girl wouldn't have minded letting the affair drift along the way it was. But it was unpleasant with Camioneto so openly her enemy. It really all started when that impresario had offered her all that money to sleep with him; it was then she realized that she was wasting her time with these two kids. She liked certain things which Luis could not give her, normal things like dresses, perfume, maybe even a little jewelry. How was he ever going to supply them when he couldn't even eat half the time? He was a flop, so why stay with him?

Now as she took off her clothes she felt a little dizzy from the drinks. She got into bed naked. Under her cold skin her blood grew warm with desire. She squirmed her naked body tight up against Luis.

Luis pulled away. "Not tonight. Relax."

Have it your way, she thought. She turned toward the wall and before closing her eyes she fell to counting the days until Sunday.

49

THEY ADDED UP THEIR MONEY. CAMIONETO
folded the dirty bills and put them in his shirt pocket.

"Fifteen pesos left, barely enough to get out of the hotel."

Luis sat hunched over disconsolately on the garden bench.
He kept pounding his fist into his hand. "If the impresario
would just give me another chance . . ."

María, with her head leaning back against the back of the
bench, laughed. "Oh sure, after Sunday he's going to give
you another chance!"

"You lay off!" Camioneto hissed. "We've heard enough
about that. He'll do better in Chihuahua."

María laughed again and said nothing. What did she care
about the future of Luis Ortega. It was Wednesday already,
practically Sunday. She had the two hundred pesos from the
man she'd dedicated the bull to still intact and that was plenty
to get her to Laredo. Before she would have been worried,
wondering what lay in wait for them around the next corner.
But that was before. Since the little talk with Rafaelillo she
felt completely apart from Luis and didn't care what happened to him.

It was hot. In front of the garden there were some open
bars swarming with North Americans. They could see them
talking, moving around in there across the street. Camioneto
studied them. An idea had been growing in his brain which,
if it paid off, would give them enough money to get to Chihuahua and see the impresario Valles. They'd never get there
in time otherwise.

"I got an idea."

"What?" asked Luis.

"We'll get some parné, easy parné."

"How?"

Camioneto pointed across the street and explained. There were lots of gringo soldiers over there, drunk, who came across the border to spend the evening in Juárez and have some fun with the muchachas. They were easy to separate from their money. Camioneto proposed they just help them a bit. They needed María for that. She'd be the bait to attract the victim. They'd invite her to go to bed and then . . .

Luis didn't let him finish.

"Not that," he said. "Count her out. And me too."

"Why?" said Camioneto soothingly. "Nothing will happen to her. It will just be pretend."

"No matter how — no."

"The idea isn't so bad," said María. She had some private embellishments to the plan. Help them lift a few dollars off a gringo all right but keep a few out for herself.

"I don't like it!" Luis said firmly. The idea of María alone with another man was what bothered him most of all.

Camioneto and María went ahead with their plans.

Furious, Luis had to accept them finally.

"Give me a cigarette," said the girl. Camioneto gave her one and she stuck it in her mouth and left it unlit. She got up and crossed the street and went into the first bar. FRANK's, said the sign over the glass front. They followed a few yards behind but stayed outside. Leaning up against the wall they could watch her out of the corner of their eyes. They saw her casually walk the length of the narrow bar, then stroll back. There was an empty stool next to one soldier. María stopped and said something to him. He pulled out his lighter and lit her cigarette for her. He was drinking and they saw the red-faced man gesture towards the stool. She sat down and the barman brought a drink.

"I don't like any part of this!" said Luis.

"She's doing fine," Camioneto answered.

When he saw her finish her eighth drink, Luis exploded: "That's it! I'm getting her out of there!"

Camioneto grabbed him. "Take it easy or I'll bust you one! Let her work . . ."

Another half hour went by. The gringo must have been very drunk, since he was resting his head on María's shoulder. From time to time his hands caressed the girl's breasts, she doing nothing more than giggle as though it tickled.

The barman brought the change from his twenty-dollar bill. The soldier left a tip, grabbed María by the waist, and staggering, they headed for the door.

"You're pretty rich," she said as they went out the door.

He nodded. "Mucho rico . . . mucho dollar . . ."

María cast a sidelong glance at Luis and Camioneto and winked at them to follow as she crossed the street with the soldier. The boys watched them go into the hotel. They saw the light of their room go on.

"Now all we do is wait," said Camioneto as he sat down on the bench.

Luis did likewise, never taking his eyes off the rectangle of light. Then the light went out.

A seemingly interminable time passed. It could have been five minutes or an hour. Luis couldn't stay still. He paced up and down and his mouth was dry. Camioneto, on the other hand, was casually reading a page torn out of an *El Ruedo*.

"God, it's taking a long time," Luis said between clenched teeth.

"Don't worry. The gringo's probably fallen asleep."

"Then what the hell are they doing?"

"How should I know!"

Luis sat on the bench in anguish. His wife, because she really was his wife, though not legally, was up there in a room with an unknown man. Alone, maybe naked on the bed. And he — like a goddamned eunuch — just sat there waiting for her to rob him of some money, money that he in his impotence hadn't been able to earn for her.

He glanced at Camioneto, who sat there bored watching the passing crowds. Luis suddenly felt a violent hate for this insensitive animal who had coldbloodedly cooked up this crooked scheme. If it weren't for him —

But just then María appeared in the entrance of the hotel. When she saw them, she crossed the street quickly.

Luis took her by the shoulders.

"What took so long?"

"The guy wouldn't go to sleep," she said, pushing back a lock of hair from her forehead.

"Did you get the parné?" asked Camioneto.

She nodded.

"Give it to me."

From the front of her blouse María took out the roll of American dollar bills. Camioneto thumbed through them quickly.

"Forty dollars. Not bad!"

With his eyes blazing Luis snapped: "You were in there about two hours! What was going on?"

María laughed. She was happy. If the boys had made forty dollars, she had made more than that, and she had it well hidden in her brassière.

"Nothing happened — nothing what you're thinking. The gringo just didn't want to go to sleep, that's all."

Her glance crossed briefly with Camioneto's, long enough

to see the mocking disbelief of her excuse in them. Luis preferred to believe it.

"Let's get out of here," he said.

"And all the capes and costumes?" said Camioneto. "Just leave them?"

"But they're in the room . . ."

"The gringo's dead asleep," María broke in. "He'll never hear you."

Camioneto started across the street. "Come on, Luis."

As they left, María decided that now was the time. She had planned to make her getaway the next day. But this was perfect. When they came back she just wouldn't be there. She could catch the four o'clock bus for Laredo.

She turned and looked up at the window of the room where they'd been staying. As she did she felt for a moment a pang of remorse, of some brief nameless fear of the future, of insecurity. But then she snapped out of it. What did they matter anyway? Everyone would be better off if she cleared out.

She spun on her heels and began to walk, slowly at first, then faster and faster down a side street.

50

LUIS AND CAMIONETO WERE ALREADY WELL into the lobby of the hotel when they saw the big soldier tucking in his shirt and bellowing at the fat desk clerk: "They robbed me — that crooked greaser dame robbed me of ninety bucks!"

The clerk had spotted them and he pointed to them.

"Those are the ones she was with!"

Luis spun and ran, shouting to Camioneto: "Beat it!"

Out the door and down the street they went. The big soldier was behind them but losing ground. "Stop them," he
kept yelling, "robbers! Help, police!"

Suddenly there appeared in front of them a wall of uniforms and they were trapped.

Thirty nights and twenty-nine days they spent in jail. They
slept in a damp cell, and were made to get up at five in the
morning to scrub the floors, rake the yard, and clean the la-
trines. Camioneto's bad leg began to go back on him until
finally he couldn't walk. He was taken to the infirmary and
given injections for a week.

It wasn't at all bad, the jail. They were given three meals
a day. Not much but regularly. The time in the infirmary
helped Camioneto put on several pounds and also to remove
the pain he'd been suffering in his hip. On the other hand
Luis was restless and wild with the inactivity and he grew
thinner. The guards were lenient and let them work out
every day with a blanket for a cape. Afterwards they would
sit up against the brown walls and wait for the days to pass.
Luis could not get over María's disappearance. She must
have gone off with someone, otherwise she would have found
a way to contact them. But he didn't want to believe it, and
thoughts of her never left his mind.

Finally the day came when they were turned loose. It was
a hot afternoon and as they stepped blinking out into the
afternoon sun Camioneto said to Luis: "Stealing's no good.
This happened because we got mixed up with other people."

They walked away from the jail fast.

Now the world was once more wide open to them. They
were alone again, as they should be, with no women getting

under foot. They shared a feeling of hunger and a craving to return, to go back to Mexico City.

"Let's get a move on," said Camioneto as they headed for the freight yards, "We only have two thousand kilometers to go!"

51

THE CITY SMELLS OF MEXICO CITY STUNG their nostrils. As they walked down hot and turbulent Bolívar Street for the first time in nearly a year, Luis felt that now at last things were going to turn out right for him.

They went in to the Café Cantonés and the Tupinamba: the same faces talking about the same things. The old Chinaman blinked at them with little surprise and Conchita was still serving the same people the same orders in the same places. It was as though the time they'd been away hadn't really existed. They joined a gang for some coffee and chatted briefly about their adventures. But there was something on Luis's mind: Juanito Lavín's mother.

As they headed for her house, Luis thought how much better and easier it would have been if he'd just bought two cents' worth of paper and written her, telling her about what had happened that terrible day and giving her Juanito's last words, those words that seemed to have been forgotten in the dusty memory of the last few months. How to begin? How to explain the long silence. Wouldn't it be easier to lie to her? "Juanito and us split up a long time ago. You mean he hasn't come back here yet?" But maybe that would be cruel to make the poor old woman go on waiting and waiting for a son who would never come back.

Along San Juan de Letrán Street the first neon signs had started blinking. There was a little circus and people milled around the entrance which gave out the metallic sounds of a band and the concentrated odor of sawdust, urine, and sweat.

In front of the wretched flat where Juanito's mother lived, Luis hesitated before knocking with a trembling hand.

"Knock again," said Camioneto.

Finally the door was opened by Juanito's mother. For a moment she studied the boys who stood there stiffly, saying nothing, and then she invited them in.

"You've come alone?" she asked as they came into the miserably furnished room. Nothing had changed since they were last there; the battered old furniture, the tattered screen of blue silk, the Ruano Llopis bullfighting prints thumbtacked to the wall. It just smelled a little damper, emptier, lonelier.

"Yes," said Luis.

There was a silence. The woman forgot to tell them to sit down. There was an air of contained expectancy and anxiety in the room. She rested one of her bony hands on the fragile table in the center of the room. From deep down in her breast came the next question:

"And Juanito? He didn't come with you?"

Camioneto chose to let his gaze go around the room as he twisted his greasy cap. Luis lowered his head and didn't take his eyes off the tips of his torn tennis shoes.

"No, señora. He — stayed there."

This seemed to satisfy the woman.

"And when will he come back? Didn't he say?"

With an ever tightening knot in his throat Luis said:

"No, he didn't say anything, because . . . he's not coming back now . . ."

There was a long silence as in a nightmare. Luis heard a groan and a little sound of pain. She knows now, he thought. He raised his head and looked at her. The mother kept looking at him, her eyes very wide, her mouth slack.

"Then," she stammered, "Juanito — he's — not coming?"

"A bull — the day after we left."

"Oh God . . ."

"A pinto bull, one that had been fought before."

"Did he suffer much?"

"Not much. And he said to tell you that he never took a backward step. The way you would want it."

Slowly she backed up to the sofa. She sagged down on it and stayed with her eyes fixed on some spot in space for several moment. Perhaps she was remembering her son's smile the day he had left.

"The way I would want it . . ." she echoed numbly.

Luis cleared his throat.

"He was a fine fellow," he said lamely. "Fine and every bit a man."

She smiled somehow. What good was it that her son was a fine fellow and every bit a man? Now Juanito didn't exist any longer. She smiled again. It was curious. The image of a handsome young man didn't appear before her tear-filled eyes now; it was a child of two or three with brown curls who ate mud in the yard and who liked to curl up in her lap to go to sleep.

"And after all this," she said suddenly, pulling herself together, "you still want to be a torero?"

"Sí señora," said Luis. "More than ever."

"You're not afraid of ending up like him?"

"He died like a real torero. At least, in his death he was a real torero. I am not one yet. And if it happens that I die that way, that's all right . . ."

Roughly, the woman grabbed Luis and shook him.

"Leave bullfighting, Luis!" she shouted. She was transformed, suddenly violent. Her thin hands had a pathetic strength. "Leave it before the bulls kill you too!"

Luis shook his head. "I can't. I've got to make it, señora. I'd rather die from a bull than hunger."

Camioneto had undone the bundle and taken out a cape. He handed it to the woman folded.

"It was his," he said simply.

"It's a little tired, señora," Luis said apologetically, "We've been using it ever since."

The woman stroked the dirty cape. "A little tired." It was more than just a dirty yellow and magenta cloth. It had been bed and shroud to her son, tool and defense to these other two boys. She handed it to Luis.

"You keep it," she said. "It is no use to me now."

Embarrassed, Luis accepted it, murmuring his thanks. Camioneto's eyes lit up at having got the cape back. He tied up the bundle again and they started to go.

"You're leaving?"

"Yes, señora."

"But you don't have a place to sleep. Stay here. You can have Juanito's cot. And there'll always be a little something to eat."

Luis wanted to say no, that they would be able to take care of themselves, but Camioneto elbowed him in the side and said: "Very pleased to accept, señora. And it won't be for long, because soon Luis will be appearing at the Plaza México . . ."

The woman walked ahead of them. "Come. The cot is over here . . ."

52

THE IMPRESARIO WAS GETTING OUT OF HIS long black Buick. They stood resolutely in front of him.

"What do you want, fellows?" he said without stopping. He was dressed nattily in gray and he smelled of Yardley. They trotted along beside him. "Well — what do you want?"

"To talk, señor."

"That's what we seem to be doing."

"Last year you said you'd give me a corrida," said Luis with a smile, "Well here I am!"

"Who are you?"

"Luis Ortega, señor."

"Well," said the impresario as he turned at the metal door in front of the corridor that led to the offices. "Come see me next year. Perhaps then there'll be . . ."

Luis broke in: "But that's what you said last year!"

"Really?" There was an edge of irritation now. "Well I'm repeating it then."

"But señor — " Camioneto grabbed the man's arm in desperation, "The matador here has been in the wars all year so you'd give him a chance! He's a great torero, I swear it, he'll cut ears, I promise . . ."

A brief smile crossed the impresario's face. "That's what they all say."

And then he was gone.

It was noon and the spring sun burned down. In big letters a poster announced the reappearance of Paco Ortiz. "At least they give somebody a chance." The scalpers were hawking tickets at five times the box office price. A pushing dark mass of people buzzed around the ticket sellers.

"You see?" Luis said bitterly, as they started walking. "It was all a lie."

"Don't get discouraged, Matador. We'll find a way."

"How do the others get in and not me?"

"Luck."

"This is like anything else. People make their own luck."

"What you need is a manager here in the city with connections."

"One like Don Paco?"

"There are others who aren't queer who are also close to the impresario."

"With them it's impossible! But with these others . . ."

"And you want one of them messing around with you?"

Luis didn't answer for a minute. He turned and Camioneto could see the hard determination in his eyes. "Well, why not? The only important thing is getting a chance to fight, no matter how."

Camioneto shook his head. "That stinks. Sure there are plenty of bums around getting by that way. But did any of the great toreros have to get to the top that way? Not one. Bullfighting's still a man's game . . . not a fairy's."

Luis pounded his fist into his hand. "I'm going to fight this season in La México! — I'm going to show you and her and — and myself what kind of a torero I am and I'm going to do it with fairies or without them, but I'm going to do it!"

They had reached Bolívar Street now. Outside the Tupinamba the same kids were hanging around as always, talking about bulls, dreaming about bulls, waiting, waiting without impatience, without hope, for some miracle to come along and make them big stars, and in the meanwhile snatching a little amusement by studying, comparing, and criticizing the

varying anatomy of passing girls. Banderilleros, sword han-
dlers, picadores, and managers were there leaning up against
the big plate glass window smoking in the sun and telling
lies to each other. Inside the café seemed dark and practically
empty.

"Go to the Cantonés," said Camioneto. "I've got an idea
I could try. I'll meet you later."

Luis went into the café and sat down in a booth in the back.
Conchita watched him come in and didn't get up from behind the counter, knowing by instinct and the look of him
that he had nothing but dust in his pockets today and wouldn't
be ordering anything. She went back to reading her magazine.

Luis put his feet on the seat and leaned back against the
wall. With his eyes closed, he sat unmoving for a long time.
María, he thought. What would she be doing now? Where?
How marvelously she made love. She had such a wonderful
slim, warm body and the smell of her could drive you wild.
If she were only here! He needed a woman so badly. If he
had money he'd go looking for one tonight on San Juan
Street. If he had money . . .

Somebody was saying: "What's up, Matador?"

He opened his eyes and sat up. A round tan face smiled
at him. It was a rather short man, dressed in a blue herring-
bone suit, whom he didn't recognize right away.

"May I?"

"Why not?"

The man sat down in front of Luis, rested his elbows deli-
cately on the table and looked at him.

"Remember me?" He smiled and displayed a gold tooth in
the center. "They call me El Nene — The Kid."

"Ah." Luis remembered him now. A manager and one of
the classic types around Bolívar Street; people said strange
things about him.

"You're Ortega aren't you? When did you get back?"

"Yesterday."

"Any photos?"

Luis extracted some from his back pocket. Murky pictures on postcard paper, they were ragged from having been taken out so many times to be shown, from having been pored over alone so much. El Nene shuffled through them, studying each one attentively.

"You've got style," he said finally, "and you've got class."

"You think so?"

"Have you seen the impresario?"

"Next year," Luis mocked. "Next year."

"That's the way it always is. You need the right manager. One who knows his way around, who knows how to push you right up there."

"That's what we want, Nene, but . . ."

"Think no more about it. I'll take over." He took out a package of cigarettes and offered one to Luis, who took it. "You and I are going to be good friends, Luis, you'll see."

Luis looked him in the eyes. Delicate, shining, unctuous, repulsive eyes. Luis wanted to get down to business, get it over with.

"Whatever you say, Nene . . ."

El Nene stood up and came over to Luis's side of the booth. Luis felt the man's little fat hand on his thigh. He felt his skin prickle under the touch of it.

"Friends, purely and simply. Just really good friends . . ."

"Whatever you say," Luis said again.

"In fifteen days I'll have you fighting in La México."

"I want to bullfight. That's all that matters."

"The hunger's got you down, hasn't it?"

"It isn't just the hunger in the stomach. There's a worse hunger up here. I've got to show what I'm made of, and I've got to do it in the biggest ring in the world."

"I'll fix it. It'll be easy."

The hand began working up. El Nene kept smiling. Luis looked back at him without blinking . . . There was a second when he felt an almost uncontrollable desire to smash this little marionette's face. But he controlled himself.

"Want to go over to my place?" El Nene said.

"Why not?" said Ortega flatly.

53

"SEEN ORTEGA?" CAMIONETO ASKED.

Without looking up from her magazine the waitress jerked her head towards the door.

"Left a while ago. With El Nene."

"With who?"

"With that maricón. He was loving up your friend in back there."

Camioneto went out fast. He went up to the Tupinamba, to the Flower of Mexico, to the Do Brasil and back to the Cantonés. Luis was nowhere about. No, no it couldn't be. He knew Luis too well to think that he'd stoop that low. But on the other hand, Luis wanted to redeem himself, to make it in La México more than anything else in the world . . .

It was four o'clock when Luis finally pushed open the café's doors and came in. Conchita smirked and glanced over at Camioneto, who ground his cigarette out in the plate in front of him.

Luis sat in the other seat. Camioneto opened his mouth but no words came out.

"What's new?" Luis asked wearily.

"That's what I say. What's new? Where'd you go?"

"I went out."

"That much I know."

"I went out."

"Alone?"

"With El Nene."

"What the hell are you doing going out with that maricón?"

Luis didn't answer. There was a sharp ache right behind his eyes and a dull one all through his body.

"So you went to mess around with him!"

Luis nodded.

"I was going to. But then I couldn't. It disgusted me. The whole thing. Nothing happened. I told him I'd rather never fight another bull anywhere than go through with it."

"Honest?"

The tears in Luis's eyes told Camioneto he was telling the truth. He reached across the table and shook his friend's hand. "I'll treat you to a veal steak. And I got some good news. Conchita, service!"

While Luis ate, Camioneto told Luis how he'd seen The Chicken earlier and arranged for Luis to fight in the town of Cuautla the next day. He would pay twenty-five pesos and expenses.

"Lots of people from here will be at the fight. If you do really well, as well as you did last time there, The Chicken says there's a good chance for La México!"

Luis's heart leapt. His luck *was* changing.

"And the bulls?"

"Piedras Negras," said Camioneto. "Rejects."

Rejects. Of course. Piedras Negras was a great ranch and their first-class bulls were wonderful to work with. But with rejects one never knew.

"It all depends on you now, Luis."
"I won't let you down this time, Pancho. I swear it."

54

WHEN HIS BULL CAME OUT, THE SECOND OF
the afternoon, Luis felt his heart give a little bump of accelera-
tion. It was a comparatively small animal, skinny, very high
of head, and with enormous horns. It pounded aimlessly
around the ring, occasionally raking the wooden fence with
its sharp points. Luis followed intensely every single move it
made, sweat glistening on his face. "Oh God, just let it charge
like the first one," he pleaded. The one The Chicken had
fought had been perfect, powerful but brave and wonderful
for the left hand. But The Chicken had not known how to
fight it, and had been soundly booed. If this one charges half
as well, Luis said to himself, I'll really show them!

Without waiting for the bull to be tested by a banderillero
Luis ran out from behind the burladero.

"Toro!" he called once. The bull charged, and Luis gave
it some wide but graceful verónicas to test its charge. His
heart sank. He could tell by the first three bucking, twisting
swerving charges that the bull was very bad and very dangerous. "It's been fought before!"

The audience was silent.

Then it was time to imitate a *quite*, to pretend to take the
bull away from the nonexistent picadors. Luis went out to
the bull, flipped the cape over his head, and held one side out
behind his legs. The bull charged. Luis held his ground, his

feet flat on the sand, and swung the cape with his right hand. The needlelike point of the horn skimmed by three inches from his waist and a great roar went up from the crowd. Luis ran after the bull, holding out the other side, like a butterfly's wing, to the animal. It charged again and this time it hooked it as it went past and Luis had to suck in his stomach and come up on his toes to keep the horn from hitting him. Another roar from the crowd. Luis knew the next would be the most dangerous of all, but he had to finish the series right.

"Toro! Ah-haaaaaa!"

The bull charged erratically again, and this time the rounded side of the horn glanced off the boy's stomach. The crowd screamed, but Luis snapped the cloth around his waist gracefully and walked back to the fence. His face was drenched in sweat and he held his side as he fought for breath, but the applause was sweet.

"It's a terrible bull!" Camioneto warned him as he handed him the water bottle and wiped off his face with the towel. Then he shoved the sword and muleta over the fence to him. "Now give him three or four punishing passes and then face-fight him. You can't do anything else with this treacherous ox so don't try!"

Luis went through the routine pantomime of asking the judge's permission to kill the animal, then ordered the helpers to get behind the fence. The bull was out in the middle of the ring. Luis looked as though hypnotized at the two horns glistening in the sunlight. He started walking out to it, the muleta held low and dragging on the sand. He stopped nine feet from the animal, and shook the muleta. The animal pawed the ground twice, and then bellowing it lunged forward, bucking and hooking from side to side. The torero bent his knee and gave it a twisting wrenching pass as he did. He repeated this six times. It was a functional maneuver and the crowd was silent in their ignorance but it was done smoothly and just the way it should have been done. The bull began to charge a little better because of the lesson it was getting, but it could not be trusted to make a really decent ordinary pass.

The crowd did not realize this. "Stand still!" they shouted. That's what they wanted to see, the pretty stuff, the horns scraping the ribcage while the man stood gracefully and arched his back and pirouetted. The fools! They didn't see that this bull didn't have one honest charge in it; Luis had extracted the few remaining ones in the first part of the fight and now there was nothing to be done but to face-fight it and prepare it for the sword thrust.

The crowd was getting nasty now. Some began throwing clods and one hit Luis in the forehead. "Damned maricón, give us some decent passes!"

Luis gritted his teeth. To hell with them! He kept working on the bull doing what he knew was proper for this bull. Camioneto signaled him from the fence that he was doing fine and it was time to kill.

But the crowd was throwing bottles now and screeching filthy insults. One bottle struck the boy in the back and made him stumble. A murmur of laughter rewarded the wielder of the missle. The pain of the bottle and a new insult bellowed down from the crowd made Luis lose his head.

"All right goddamn it I'll show them!" His head was buzzing with pain and rage. The bull was eight feet away and Luis, the muleta in his right hand, began edging up sideways to it. His rage against his luck and the crowd was all concentrated on the animal and he shook the cloth angrily and defiantly, his feet flat on the sand.

"No, Luis!" Camioneto was calling. "No!"

Luis shook the muleta again. "Come on you goddamn ox!"

The bull dipped its head twice and then shook it and pawed

the ground. Luis felt no fear at all now, only irrepressible anger. He would show them that he was a torero and a man, a brave man who shouldn't be insulted by clods and bottles when he was doing the best he knew how.

And then suddenly he saw the bull lunging forward in a hard charge, saw it heading straight for him. He saw it and didn't try to move out of the way.

"That's it," he had time to shout, almost jubilantly, "Charge me bull . . ."

He felt something crash into his right knee. No pain, only the blow. And over him there passed hide and hoofs, and a mass of black muscle, cruel and immense and infuriated. Dimly he heard screams and curses around him.

Someone was lifting him up by the armpits. Luis struggled violently.

"Let me alone, let me back at him!"

"He's given it to you!" he heard Camioneto saying, "He's given it to you!"

Then suddenly he grasped the meaning of the words, the terrible words. He looked down at his leg. From it was pumping a steady red stream that Camioneto was trying to stop with his hands. "He's given it to you!"

Now he didn't try to struggle. Something soft and dizzying was enveloping him. He passed out. Camioneto and two of the helpers picked him up and rushed him out toward the big corral in back. Great splashes of blood in the sand marked the path they took.

The stands murmured in consternation. Tragedy! The barabaric attraction of la fiesta brava. The other toreros were going to follow Luis out of the ring, but the judge's trumpet blew announcing the continuing of the corrida.

With his face green with fear, The Chicken took up Luis's muleta and sword and went out to kill the bull.

55

THEY SHOVED TWO PILES OF HAY TOGETHER
and laid him on it. He was very pale and beads of sweat
ringed his face. His eyelids fluttered and he sunk his finger-
nails deep into Camioneto's arm.

"Big — one?"

Camioneto tried to keep the fear out of his eyes. "I don't
think so."

The other toreros stared whitefaced as the blood from the
wound kept up its unchanging rhythm.

"Give me a handkerchief!" Camioneto ordered.

One of them drew out a dirty bandanna from his pocket.
Camioneto took one end in his teeth, passed the other around
Luis's leg above the wound and then tied it tight. The wound
still bled, drenching the hay under the limp body.

"Got to get a doctor!" Camioneto set off at his fastest limp-
ing run towards the village's main street, asking people as he
went where the doctor lived. Some didn't answer, some didn't
know. Finally a man pointed to a yellow house. Camioneto
ran to it and pounded on the door. After a while the door
opened and a pale and completely bald head was stuck out.

"Are you the doctor?"

"What do you want?"

"There's a man wounded! Gored — come quick!"

"A torero?"

"He's dying in the plaza de toros!"

"I can't go."

"But Luis is dying!"

"Get the ring doctor."

"There is no ring doctor!"

"He should be there. I can't meddle in a colleague's practice. Look around for him."

The man shut the door.

Camioneto stayed frozen for a moment, not knowing what to do. "Mierda!"

There must be a hospital. He stopped a woman passing by. "Where's the hospital?"

Two blocks over and one street up. He ran hard and his shirt was wet and stuck to his skin when he came panting up to the man behind the desk. He could hardly get the words out.

"Friend — gored — come quick to the plaza! Dying!"

The man, who was in his bathrobe, took out a cigarette and lit it before answering. "They're all out."

"But he's dying!"

"And what am I supposed to do? I'm just the intern in charge."

"Then you come!"

"I can't just up and leave."

"Money? Is it money? We can fix that!"

The man smiled. "No, it's not that. Look. Bring him here and we'll see what we can do."

When Camioneto got back to the plaza the audience was leaving. He ran to the corral in back. There was a crowd standing around Luis now. Without being asked people would come up and look for a few moments, and then toss down a few coins before moving away.

Luis was so still that at first Camioneto thought he was already dead. He bent down and listened to the faint beating of his heart.

"All right," he ordered the other toreros. "Grab the ends of that cape — make a stretcher!"

They eased him onto the big cape and then started carrying him towards the village as fast as they dared go. They couldn't go too fast because every rough movement caused a new flood of blood. Already it was pooling in the sag of the cape; drops were seeping through the cloth and leaving a red trail on the cobblestones of the street.

Suddenly Luis said, without opening his eyes: "Remember, Camioneto . . . ?"

"Shhh, don't talk!"

"Camioneto — you — you remember how Juanito — how we carried — him — like this . . ."

"Don't try to talk."

"Camioneto — I'm through — I think I'm dying now . . ."

Tears were streaming down Camioneto's ugly face. "Don't talk crazy! We're coming to the hospital right now."

The intern, still in his bathrobe, was leaning up against the door waiting for them. When the toreros came in he pointed to a room with an operating table in the middle.

"Put him in there."

Calmly the man lit another cigarette, took two puffs, and then put it on the edge of the table. Without washing his hands, he began to explore the injury. He inserted his middle and index finger completely into the wound and began to feel around. Luis gave a sharp cry, and they could hear his teeth grind together.

"Hurt?" said the intern. "Afraid it's going to hurt more."

The toreros watched as the doctor worked. One grew very white and withdrew to the patio where they could hear him vomiting. The intern cut away Luis's pantlegs with some scissors. With the same scissors he began trimming the torn ragged flesh around the wound.

It was then Luis fainted.

"Doctor," cried Camioneto, "I think he's gone!"

The intern lifted one of Luis's eyelids and took his pulse. "Fainted. All the better."

Then without speaking he tied up the torn veins and arteries, cleaned the wound with alcohol, and sprinkled it with sulfa drugs. He filled in the hole with gauze, and closed the wound tightly with adhesive tape.

"All right, now get him out of here."

"But, Doctor," Camioneto protested, "how can we move him this way?"

"I've done all I can."

"Please let him stay!"

"Impossible. He can't stay here. If the bosses found out I'd done a first-aid case in here I'd be through. Get him to Mexico City or wherever you're going soon. He needs an operation."

"But wouldn't he die on the way?"

The intern shrugged his shoulders. "I really couldn't say. He may and he may not. With a little luck . . ."

They finally found a taxi driver who agreed to take them to Mexico City for sixty pesos. This was all the money the toreros had.

They placed Luis as comfortably as possible in the back seat. He had come out of the faint now and he moaned continually. The Chicken and two of the other toreros sat up next to the driver who never stopped saying he wished he'd never agreed to take them. Since the taxi was overloaded and the tires were old its owner drove very slowly, ignoring Camioneto's pleas to go faster.

"Better late than to break down on the way," he kept muttering.

It was two o'clock in the morning before they finally drove into the city. The streets were deserted and the neon signs were all out. They lost another fifteen minutes trying to find the Sanatorio de Toreros.

At last they pulled up in front of a door lit by a bright lantern.

"This is it."

Camioneto and The Chicken went in. A sleepy nurse asked him what they wanted.

"We've got a man wounded out here in the car. Got it in Cuautla."

"Name?"

"Luis Ortega. Hurry."

"In the Union?"

Camioneto stammered, "Not yet."

"Then," said the girl, stifling a yawn, "can't let him in."

"But he's a torero!"

"Can't help it."

"Look — is this the Sanatorio de Toreros?"

"Yes."

"It's for healing wounded toreros?"

"Naturally."

"Well, I got one here! Heal him!"

"I'm sorry I can't do a thing."

"For the love of God, señorita, just for tonight! This boy could die!"

"I'm sorry, boys. I just work here. I'd be fired."

The Union — could anything be more ridiculous — Luis was going to die because of a lousy dues-gobbling syndicate!

The Chicken pulled Camioneto away, but not before he had fastened his tear-filled eyes on the woman and said, "You and your goddamn Union go screw yourselves!"

At the driver's suggestion they went next to Red Cross.

Down a nightmare of corridors they ran and finally found themselves in front of a man sitting at a desk, a man who stared dully at them through his thick glasses.

"We got a wounded man — "

"What happened to him?"

"Gored — in Cuautla today. . . ."

The man tilted his chair back against the wall. "Cuautla, you say?"

"Yes, he's a novillero."

The man locked his fingers behind his head.

"Can't take him."

"Why, for God's sake?"

"Happened in Cuautla — outside the Federal District."

"But he's dying out there!"

The man tapped his teeth with a pencil. "I'm sorry but I didn't make the rules. You should have left him in Cuautla."

"For the love of God, señor. . . ."

"You toreros have your own hospital, don't you? Take him there. I honestly can't help you here."

As they left an ambulance was skidding into the driveway.

"Now what," Camioneto asked hoarsely of the world in general, "Now what do we do?"

"We could try old Doctor Ibarra," said The Chicken suddenly. "I just thought of him!"

"He'll probably be like all the rest."

"Not him," said The Chicken. "He'll be mad as hell, though, when we wake him up."

56

THEY HAD BEEN WAITING FOR TWO HOURS.
A cold and dirty light was beginning to come through the
window, making the walls of the room gray. They were sep-
arated from the operating room by an opaque glass wall.
Once again Camioneto got up and paced to the door, behind
which Doctor Ibarra was operating.

"Take it easy," said The Chicken.

"Why's he taking so long?"

Camioneto dropped onto the bench and picked up the copy
of *The Arena* newspaper. He leafed through it for the third
time, not seeing the pictures or reading the words.

"They give it a big spread, don't they," said The Chicken.

"What?" said Camioneto dully.

"The scratch Paco Ortiz got in La México." The Chicken
pointed to the headlines. "Grave goring — " He laughed.
"Five lousy little centimers and they call it grave. And here's
Luis with — "

"Luis is a nobody. Ortiz is in style now. He could scratch
his finger and he'd get more publicity than Luis would if —
if he — died."

He got up and started pacing again. Then the door opened
and Doctor Ibarra appeared. He was a tall reedy man who
gave the impression that he might snap in two at any moment.
But his smiling eyes were steely and strong. He looked tired
now and his bony face was drawn and blue with whiskers.
He lit a cigarette.

"How is he, Doctor?"

"Terrible. What the devil did that man do to him?"

"Will he make it?"

"Luckily the bull knew his anatomy. The horn slipped between the main arteries and didn't hurt them. A little bit one way or the other . . ."

"But he'll make it?"

"Month in bed at least. But he'll make it, if there are no complications."

Camioneto swallowed. "And you won't throw him out of here before the month is up?"

"Now why would I do that?"

"No money to pay you."

"Who's talking about money?" growled Ibarra. "He can pay me back when he's a big star. But for Christ's sake don't tell anybody or I'll have them all in here."

When they went out to get some coffee, a pale sun was out trying to cast shadows on the pavement.

"That's great about Ibarra," said The Chicken, "but what about the room. How you going to pay for that?"

"Don't you think I'm worrying about that? I've been thinking and thinking and I don't know anywhere to get the parné."

"What about some big torero? They're usually decent about a loan for something like this."

"Oh sure, I've got dozens of big toreros for friends."

"How about Garza? Didn't you say he bailed Luis out once?"

Lorenzo Garza! That was it! But how to find him?

"They'll know at the Tupinamba," said The Chicken. "They know everything in the Tupi."

57

A SERVANT TOLD HIM THAT THE MATADOR
had not arisen yet.

"I'll wait," said Camioneto, and he sat on a bench in the garden.

The bells had just chimed eight o'clock. The air was moist and cool. Soon the sun would be scorching. He lit up a cigarette and tried to wait patiently. Around nine, the garage door opened and a Cadillac backed out. Camioneto saw that Lorenzo Garza himself was at the wheel.

"Good morning, Matador," he said taking off his cap.

"Hello, lad." He had his characteristic long cigar jutting from a corner of his mouth. "What do you want?"

"I've come to ask a favor — "

"Come back at noon. I'm in a hurry . . ."

"It's about Luis Ortega. A bull got him Sunday."

"Who in God's name is Luis Ortega?"

Camioneto reminded him of the favor he'd done Luis in Jalostotitlán.

"So that's Ortega."

"Yes, Matador, and we need help."

"Well. Get in. I have to see a building I'm putting up and then maybe we'll see what we can do."

A large group of boys surrounded Garza's car as they pulled up in front of the clinic. The doors were opened from the outside for them and there were hero-worshipping greetings from the crowd as the matador made his way to the door.

Inside there were half a dozen newspapermen and photographers, and they clustered around. Garza, elegant in his
sport coat and silk scarf, smiled affably and shook hands with
all of them.

"You've come to see Ortiz, eh?" said the big critic of *Esto*,
Juan de Triana.

Garza hooked his index finger around the cigar and took it
from his mouth. "Luis Ortega."

"Who the hell is he?"

Garza glanced at Camioneto and smiled. "Friend of ours."

"Never heard of him, Matador."

"You will, boys. Remember the name."

Camioneto led the way proudly to Luis's room, and held
the door open for Garza.

The room was darkened, just a little light leaking through
the venetian blinds. The smell of medicine and antiseptics
was sharp. Over the bed was a metal crucifix. As they closed
the door Garza took the cigar out of his mouth. Luis was
drowsing.

"Luis," Camioneto called softly. "The matador is here."

Ortega stirred. He was full of sedatives. With difficulty he
opened his eyes. He recognized Camioneto bending over him.
He heard a far-off voice, vaguely familiar saying: "Let's let
him sleep. I'll come back later."

"He's awake now, Matador."

Luis ran his tongue over his dry lips. It was hot.

"Who — is — it?"

"El matador Lorenzo Garza!" Camioneto put his arm
around Luis's shoulders and helped him sit up a bit.

"How goes it, boy?"

Luis recognized the unmistakable big nose and smiling face
of the torero, and he managed a pale smile in return.

"Fine, Matador. . . ."

"So, they really gave it to you."

"Yes, Matador. For just standing there like a fool . . ."

Garza said nothing. His jaws worked as he looked at the boy, as though remembering his own hungry, painful beginnings so long ago. He was looking at himself there in the bed.

"Has it been rough, boy?"

"Just a scratch, Matador," said Luis, and then he smiled at himself and the ridiculousness of what he'd said, and Garza smiled with him.

"The first one's the bad one."

"It isn't the wound that hurts so much, Matador." Luis got himself on to his elbows feebly. "It's not being able to get a fight in La Plaza México. I got to get out of here soon and get back to the bulls."

"You take it easy." Garza smiled. He liked this boy who was still nauseated from a major operation and yet who was already planning how he could get back in front of the horns. "I've seen you fight, Luis Ortega, and I've seen you work in close and with style. You'll be a matador, and a good one." He turned to Camioneto. "The impresario is out there talking to the newspapermen. Tell him I want to see him."

When Camioneto had hurried out, Garza took out his wallet, extracted several bills, and put them on the dresser. "The room is all taken care of for as long as necessary, but here's a little extra."

There were tears in Luis's eyes. "I don't need the money, Matador — I eat three times a day here. Much better would be if there was some way to get me a fight . . ."

Camioneto came in followed by three men. They stood around the bed after Garza had shaken hands with them.

"Luis, here you have the impresario of La México." Garza rubbed his hands together. "Now we're going to do battle with him!"

The impresario put a friendly arm around the matador's shoulders. "What's the problem?"

"Just that we want you to sign this boy up for a corrida. He's got class and he's got guts. What more do you want?"

"Well, we can talk about that sometime."

"We can talk about it right now. This boy is my protégé and you're not leaving the room without giving us a definite date!"

"What about it?" said the newspaperman, smiling. The photographer was already taking a photograph of Luis, who had sagged back on the bed weakly.

58

THREE KNOCKS CAME ON THE DOOR. CAMI-oneto put down his newspaper and went to the door. Through the little peephole he saw it was a woman.

"Who is it?" asked Luis from his bed.

"Nobody," said Camioneto, leaving the room.

"What do you want?" he said, not closing the door all the way but blocking the entrance.

"I want to see him. I heard what happened . . ."

"Why didn't you come when he was really sick if you were going to come? He's just a few days from getting out now."

"I couldn't — believe me."

Camioneto folded his arms. "You'd better go. He doesn't want to see you."

"I just want to see him for a minute . . ."

Luis was calling. "Who is it?" In his heart he was hoping, praying for it to be María.

Camioneto went back in the room and the woman slipped in behind him.

Luis's heart gave a skip.

The girl smiled sadly. "Me."

"Estela!"

He stared at the shabbily dressed girl. She had grown old in only a year. Her face was lined and her hair unkempt. A light beige coat could not hide her thinness. They kept looking at each other for a long time without saying anything. Camioneto went out.

"How are you?" Luis finally said, immersed in the memory of that long-passed time. He held his hand out to her. Estela took it in both of hers. Her skin was rough now, not like before.

She began to cry; actually she had been crying since she came into the room and saw Luis pale in the bed.

"Fine," she said tenderly. "And you."

"Well, as you can see — I'm in the repair shop."

She sat on the edge of the bed. "And otherwise, how's the world treating you?"

"I can't complain," he said proudly. "I've got a definite date for La Plaza México."

"I'm so glad, Luis!"

They soon realized that they had nothing to talk about. She had been so important to him once; now he felt nothing for her, except perhaps a certain remote gratitude for having helped him when he needed it."

"And you, Estela? What are you doing these days?"

"What would I be doing?"

"I thought maybe things had changed."

"Nothing changes. One day is like the next."

"Maybe it's better that way."

She stood up to go, and Luis felt relief. Although she hadn't stayed five minutes he was tired from the effort. She took one of his hands and pressed it to her with real affection.

"I'm very glad you came," Luis said and he said it sincerely.

"Thank you, Luis." She kissed him on the forehead and he smelt the perfume and alcohol.

To say something, Luis said: "I'll be seeing you when I get out."

She knew he wouldn't. "Wonderful, Luis."

Camioneto was in the hallway looking out the window as she came out and went passed him, her shoulders drooping wearily. He went back into the room and opened a window to let the cheap perfume out.

"Well, what did she want?"

"Just to say hello."

"What'd she really want? Get back together?"

"No, just to see me."

"It's your business, but if you start to get . . ."

"Dry up and hand me a glass of water!"

As Camioneto poured the water into the glass he saw a folded bill on the bureau. He picked it up.

"And this?"

"Where'd that come from?"

Camioneto handed it to Luis.

"One hundred pesos!"

Luis handed it back, shaking his head incredulously.

Camioneto folded it up and put it in his pocket.

"We're doing fine — this plus Garzas'." Then he added: "I guess she was better than most buñís."

59

AT THIS HOUR, THE TUPINAMBA WAS LIKE A market place. People were talking about soccer and bullfighting. In one corner a group of Spaniards sounded off against Franco. Through the blue curtain of smoke they found an unoccupied table. There was an infernal racket, a mixture of voices, shouts, orders, laughter, and plates clattering against each other. It reeked of tobacco, of people crowded together, of a café in general.

"Over there," said Camioneto, pointing.

Some people greeted Luis, wishing him luck on Sunday. Others simply smiled or slapped him on the shoulders. It's nice like this, he thought. It really was. Cano's coverage, the article with the photos and sweet words, had seen to it that no one in the bullfighting world could help but know who Luis Ortega was. People who didn't even know who he was before now tried to ingratiate themselves with him. It was nice. But best of all had been the two weeks on the ranch of San Diego de los Padres. Two unbelievable weeks of doing nothing but eating and fighting calves under the stern eye of Lorenzo Garza. Luis trained with literally dozens of two-year-old animals, and he learned more from Garza in those fourteen days than he had the entire past year. He was sorry Garza had had to go off to Tijuana to fight and would miss Sunday's corrida.

Someone stopped Camioneto.

"What's up, Pancho, got a job for me?"

"We're all squared away, Flaco," Camioneto said off-handedly. "If only you'd come around yesterday. Anyway, there'll be a next time."

The smile still clung to the banderillero's lips.

"All right, but make it next time for sure."

"Sure."

They sat down at their own table. Around them the same bunch were busy telling each other the same lies.

The waitress came up and they ordered two coffees. Luis was beginning to get nervous. Usually on Friday night, Sunday afternoon was still a long way off, still very remote. Something that would never come. But now it was different. He already was going through the anguish of four in the afternoon on Sunday. He'd been sleeping badly for several nights. He'd awake with a start, his face and body bathed in sweat, positive that he was already out there in front of the horns in his suit of lights. Then he could never get back to sleep. Would the twenty-seventh ever come?

What a tremendous responsibility he had now. This Sunday would be a different Sunday, the decisive one in his life. Every time he saw his name on the posters on the corners he felt the icy clutch of fear in his groin and behind his ears. He found himself living an unreal existence. He enjoyed having people in the street call him by name, having unknown people as well as friends wish him luck, promising to go to the fight to watch him; it swelled his ego that his own gang around the Cantonés envied him his luck and would ask for just another look at that piece of paper where the impresario was actually committed to pay one thousand pesos. All this was wonderful, really wonderful. But the other — the sleep-robbing terror, the fear of being alone, the ever increasing nervousness — oh God!

"Hola, fellows!" he heard someone saying beside him.

He turned to see who was speaking. It was a very well dressed man, tall, thin, with gray hair. He remembered having seen him many times hanging around the cafés with toreros.

"How you feeling, Matador?" said the stranger.

"Sharp — got an edge on me like a puntilla dagger."

"The way you should be." He placed his manicured hands on the table. He went straight to the point.

"I was looking for you to set up everything for the radio and the press."

Puzzled, Luis looked at Camioneto. Pancho pushed his chair back.

"Fine, only we're not getting paid much for — "

"Doesn't matter. You've got to take care of the press. Since your boy's a beginner he's going to need a big send-off. You know — cover up if he's bad, build up if he's good. What you get paid?"

"Thousand. But we got expenses. Uniform, hotel, all that — "

"You'll have some left over." He took out a little notebook, found a page and looked over what had been written there. "Between radio, newspapers, and magazines, it'll come to seven hundred pesos. That's taking into consideration that the kid's unknown and we're trying to help him. Now, if things turn out the way they should — "

"Seven hundred's an awful lot — "

"It's nothing, really. Lalo and Juanito pay five times that every week."

"Yes, but look what they get paid!"

"I'm telling you, your boy's getting a special price. Now, if you don't want to — " his voice trailed off significantly, threateningly.

Camioneto gave a forced smile.

"No, it's not that," Camioneto hesitated. "All right."

He received a pen, paper, and a smile from the gray gentleman. The paper was in the form of a promissory note, like the one he'd signed for the uniform.

The man blew on the ink, folded the paper, and put it in his wallet as he stood up.

"Well," he said to Luis, "let's have some luck, eh?"

They watched the man's elegant presence withdraw. He stopped at another table briefly and then left. Camioneto and Luis remained silent. Luis was the first to speak.

"I don't get it. If you're good in the fight, why do you need it?"

Camioneto snorted. Luis had a lot to learn.

"They're worse than the bull. They can annihilate a torero."

"But it isn't right."

"But that's the way it is."

Camioneto added up their expenses: For the rental of the suit of lights, the dress cape, the swords, and all the rest, they only had three hundred pesos. And then there was the hotel, the food, the car to go to the plaza in. There'd be a couple of pesos left, maybe.

"And the photographers! We got to buy at least six dozen, because if you don't they'll see that the worst get published."

"Son of a bitch." Luis managed a laugh. "We go a year without eating so that we can get this fight. Now I'm going out there and maybe get hung up on a horn, and I'll come out in debt. Great business, bullfighting!"

They started to leave.

"It isn't easy, Matador," Camioneto said. "But when you make it, when you're a star, you'll have thousand-peso bills in stacks."

They finished eating, paid the bill, and started to leave.

"Hola, Ortega!"

They were near the door when a woman's voice spoke in a smiling, mocking tone. Luis whirled around. His heart had begun to pound inside his chest. He felt himself go pale.

"Say hello at least."

It was María — María Valente.

He tried to smile.

"Hola, María."

At the table there were three or four men. He couldn't have recognized them — his eyes could not seem to focus on anything. He took a step forward on trembling legs. His mouth was dry and his tongue seemed to choke him.

When he came up to the table he leaned against the back of a chair. Camioneto had kept going and Luis could see him out of the corner of his eye standing in the doorway.

One of the men held out his hand.

"Don't you say hello to old friends?"

Luis glanced at him.

"How goes it, Rafaelillo?"

Luis kept looking at María. She had changed. She was a little heavier, more womanly. Her face was too painted; it wasn't the way it had been — fresh and clean and as clear as water. Underneath the coat of powder it was rather tired and fragile. She was wearing a low-cut dress the color of bougain-villaea. Draped casually over the back of her chair was a flashy silver fox fur.

"Sit down, Luisito," she invited him.

"Thanks — I was just leaving."

He was recalling in these moments the happenings in that large chunk of his life that was María. He remembered that night in Ciudad Juárez when she had gone off without a trace, he relived the days in jail, made even more terrible by the jealous gnawings of not knowing where she was or with whom. He couldn't forget the nights when he hadn't closed his eyes once, calling her name out in the dark silence. All this came back, in a rush, upon seeing her.

A thousand questions rushed to his mind. There were so many to be answered. Why didn't he speak? Why did he keep watching her smile without opening his mouth to ask all the things he wanted to know? He'd imagined that this scene would take place so many times, it didn't matter where or how or when. But it had to happen. But he had imagined things would be different, in a simpler, more natural way. Then he would demand explanations, he would beg for some story that he'd know beforehand was false. If the tale was any good at all he'd skip the details and believe it. Maybe they could go back to what was interrupted that night, the way they used to be.

But no. Things weren't as before. He and she — they had changed since then. She wasn't the same frightened girl he'd met way back there in the truck, nor the little animal who burned with desire and gave herself to him, asking nothing in return. And he — wasn't he different?

"So you're fighting Sunday?" she asked.

"Yes," he nodded. "Sunday — "

"I'm very pleased, Luisito." She said it sincerely. "Really."

He shrugged, trying to be casual.

"Who knows how it'll turn out?"

She put her hand on the one he was leaning on the chair. He looked down. On her ring finger shone a large bluish aquamarine.

"It will turn out wonderfully — you'll see."

Rafaelillo offered him a cigarette, which he refused. As he tapped one on the table he said pointedly: "How does María look to you after so long?"

"Fine," he said without changing his expression.

"I thought you'd be asking a lot of questions, Luis — registering a few complaints."

"Me? Why?"

"Well, since she used to be yours . . ."

"That's all over."

"Didn't you look for her even?"

"No."

"Didn't you even wonder what she'd done or where she'd gone?"

"No," said Luis, and he made himself look at her. "She always knew what she was doing. I realized that the night she took off."

Rafaelillo removed the ash off his cigarette by brushing it along the inside of a glass which had contained coffee.

"You know she's not in bullfighting anymore. Got a better job now. Right, pigeon?"

The pigeon nodded.

"She's a real star."

"Really?"

"But really. She's the favorite at The Bandit's."

Luis received this news as though he'd been hit with a stick across his face. He didn't know what to say for several moments. At the Bandit's! Everybody knew that the Bandit's was the favorite house of the rich and influential. He collected himself and tried to feign indifference.

"When you get a hundred pesos," Rafaelillo was getting such pleasure out of it in front of his friends, "come around and see her."

"I will," Luis stammered, but immediately realized he had said something he didn't mean to. He blushed deeply.

"But don't ask for María Valente. She's called Mapy now."

With a hoarse voice, Luis repeated: "Mapy . . ."

"I'm her manager."

María suddenly became very nervous. She kicked her lover under the table, saying that she thought he ought to ask for the check. She knew Luis Ortega, and guessed what was going on inside him. She'd seen him go pale and she was afraid he'd lose control of himself.

"How's the parné situation?" María said.

"Fine," Luis answered.

"Here." She'd taken some bills from her purse and held them out to him.

He shrank back. She insisted.

"Take them. They'll help with the expenses."

"No, thank you . . ."

He turned and left without a word more. His ears were buzzing and his blood was boiling. "Whore!" He saw everything so clearly now, everything in correct proportion. And it was better that it happened this way, brutally. There'd been a moment when he could have slipped back to loving her — now he was grateful for the cruelty of it.

The warm air in the street went deep in his lungs. It gave him a new and powerful feeling to breathe it. It was like cleaning out the dust and cobwebs inside his body. He was almost happy.

"Let's get some rest, Camioneto. Got to be in good shape . . ."

Camioneto fell into step with Luis. He was whistling a gay mariachi tune.

60

CAMIONETO SOFTLY OPENED THE DOOR. THE room in the Hotel Pennsylvania, out of which so many toreros had come and gone on to glory, was almost completely dark.

"What's up?" Luis was not sleeping.

"It's the time, Matador."

The Time! Camioneto opened the door so some air could get in. Luis sat on the edge of the bed, with his head in his hands. "The Time!" There was an alarm clock on the bureau. The hands said five minutes of three. The time was here, the time he never thought would come. Thousands of people would be arriving at the plaze de toros to see him. Thousands of people who would either applaud him to fame, or shove him into oblivion with their indifference. Ortega stayed there on the edge of the bed, naked and filled with fear. "It's good it's finally come," he said, trying to encourage himself. There was a great void in the pit of his stomach. When he rubbed one against the other he realized his feet were frozen, that his whole body was cold and heavy.

In the morning he'd gone to the Villa de Guadalupe with Camioneto, the classic ritual for a young torero. He had some boiled eggs and orange juice early. Afterwards he tried to rest in bed for a few hours. He couldn't close his eyes without strange dreams. One second he'd see himself being carried out of the ring on the shoulders of the delirious crowd — and the next he'd be stretched out on the sand, his face bloody and the Cuautla wound opened up in his thigh.

But the time was here now. Camioneto had said it. The clock had said it.

"Take a bath, Matador."

He got under the shower. The water was freezing, but somehow it didn't matter. His body felt only fear. He shuddered lightly when his fingers went over the still young scar of the goring. Then he shaved the few whiskers he had.

Camioneto had placed the folded pants of the suit of lights on the bed. He liked that salmon-colored uniform which had belonged to the great Carlos Arruza, and which Nacho Isunza now rented out. It's been around, that suit, he thought as he saw it. After the artificial pigtail was pinned on, he drew on the pink stockings. He was glad he was alone in the room, no one but Camioneto. "When I get back," he smiled deep inside, "there'll be plenty of people here."

He put his thin legs into the tight pants. El Flamenco and the Blind Muñoz came in and watched how Camioneto worked the torero's thighs into the gold-encrusted suit.

"How do we feel?" asked Muñoz.

'With his face very pale, Luis answered: "Fine."

"Seen the bulls, Matador?"

"No. I'll see enough of them later."

El Flamenco rounded out a cigarette before lighting it.

"They're beauties. Very even and comfortable, all six of them."

"And the pair you drew," added Muñoz, "they're the best of the lot."

"That's what Camioneto said."

Then Alejandro Alvárez and two fellows Luis had never seen before came in. After saying hello they distributed themselves around the room. Camioneto kept his eyes on them as though afraid they might steal something.

"The shirt — "

Bent towards the mirror, Luis knotted the shiny red tie. All he wanted was to be left alone. The presence of friends bothered him and kept him from giving in completely to his fear. It couldn't really blossom in front of them — he had to appear calm and strong.

Camioneto cinched up the knee tassels. The cords dug deep into the flesh of Luis's calves, and the painful sensation, far from bothering him, proved that he could still feel, that he was still *he*. He began to get irritable.

"For Christ's sake, you going to take all day?" he snarled

at Camioneto, who was fussing with the bows on the heelless shoes.

Camioneto said nothing, pretending not to have heard the explosion, and kept doing his work. The torero was almost dressed. It had been some time since anyone had spoken. In the hot, narrow room, one heard only the breathing. Luis looked at the watch. Three twenty-five.

"The sash . . ."

He wrapped the red silk serpent tightly around his waist.

"Too tight?" Camioneto inquired before tying it.

"No. Go ahead."

Then El Flamenco took out a flask of rum and held it out. "A swallow, Matador?"

Luis's mouth was dry as he said: "No. The vest!"

He put it on. Only the jacket remained. Camioneto took it off the back of the chair and held it out with both hands by the inside of the collar. Luis finished combing his hair and straightening the pigtail.

"You, Gallego," Camioneto ordered, "find a taxi for us. And you — " he said to El Flamenco, " — get out the sheath with the swords and the capes, and the towel and the bottle of water."

El Gallego Alvárez went to do his job. The rest of them, standing stiff and silent, waited for the final ceremony of the ritual: the putting on of the jacket. Luis put his arms into the stiff shiny sleeves. Camioneto humped the heavy gold garment well up on his shoulders. As he let it settle down, he slapped Ortega on the back.

"Que haya suerte," he wished in the classic way. "Let there be luck!"

El Flamenco and Camioneto carried the things out of the room while Luis knelt with one knee on the floor, before the little image of the Virgin of the Macarena.

"Bring me luck!" was all his lips could say.

He came out with his montera hat in his hands and the dress cape slung over his arm. The hotelkeeper, an old Spaniard, rasped with his stale cigar breath: "You better cut off the bull's ears or I'll cut yours off."

"That," Luis replied very seriously, "is what I intend to do."

He smiled and gave Luis a pat.

The car that El Gallego had brought was waiting at the door of the hotel. From the windows of the neighboring houses there sprouted clusters of heads watching the torero. Luis waited until the belongings were packed in the car. As they started off, Camioneto whispered: "Matador, I've got only five pesos — enough to get us to the plaza but not enough to bring us back."

Luis's eyes fixed on Insurgentes Avenue stretching out ahead of him.

"We don't need any more," Luis Ortega said between clenched teeth. "They're either going to carry me back on their shoulders or they're bringing me back in an ambulance."

Camioneto shuddered seeing his face when he said it.

From the cuadrillas' patio, through the cold dark tunnel, he could see a section of the stands. It was impossible to make out faces or bodies; it was just a moving splotch of brilliant color. The costumed constable clopped his horse down the passageway and the matadors, banderilleros, the picadors and the ring servants followed him. There was the excitement in the air that always comes in that nervous minute before four in the afternoon.

The cuadrilla gate was still closed. He was introduced to the other youths he was to perform with. They were wearing expensive new uniforms which made his look pale and shabby by contrast.

It isn't the suit that does the fighting, he told himself.

Old Doctor Ibarra came around. He scratched his neck and smiled at him.

"Go out there and really work close to the horns, lad. After all, you know you've got free medical service here."

Strangely, the rough joke gave him courage and he was grateful.

"Yes, Doctor."

His heart stopped pounding for a second and then started again, harder, when they swung back the gate. Luis put on his montera, shoving it down level with his eyebrows. He looked up at the stands. There wasn't a single vacant seat in the largest bull ring in all the world. Once I said I would fill this place up, he thought. And now by God I've done it and no one here is going to be sorry he came.

Someone shouted: "Get ready to go!"

Luis heard himself murmur. "Never a backward step!" as he and the other two matadors took their places at the head of their men. Then he remembered to take off his hat since he was making his first appearance in this plaza de toros.

At that moment, the chime of the clock of the Plaza México struck four times.

"*The time!*"

The band blared out suddenly and the crowd roared. And Luis Ortega took his first step into the future.